SILVER AND BLOOD

IRWIN BLACK

Cover design by Samuel and Sean Black

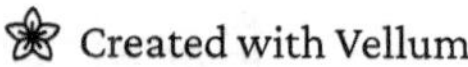 Created with Vellum

PROLOGUE

As any well-learned writer knows, it is always best to launch your story at just the point when the trouble begins. But Virginia City was always a home to trouble, and so I shall pen my tale around the particular calamitous events that nearly brought hellfire and brimstone down upon that settlement.

Now you may accuse me of hyperbole, and I will confess to embroidering details in one or two of my former works, in an effort to increase circulation. There is value in that, as you are aware. But for this submission, I attest and swear to you on a pouch of gold that what I write now is the bald truth.

You know that I have often penned my doubts in the existence of divine providence. What I do not doubt, though, is the reality of the devil incarnate. I have seen the beast with my own eyes. A serpent garbed in human raiment, devouring the flesh and souls of those in its grasp and laying waste to any resisting.

I was witness to most of the following or heard and recorded the words directly from the lips of the actors on both sides of the cataclysm. My memory is true, and my mind is sound.

With this explanation and pledge, I will conclude my preface and begin my hero's journey.

2

S. Clemens, 1864

CHAPTER

ONE

William Bancroft was almost home. One more day's ride and he would once again be on his father's homestead, eating his mother's stew and gearing up for a day of darkness, working his family's claim, that is, if his father would accept the confession of the prodigal and take him back into the fold.

It had been silver that had steered young Will's life to this point. Old Man Tibner had found a deep ribbon of gold on his site and stirred up the whole city. At that time, Virginia City was little more than a cluster of homesteaders, sharing a general store and telegraph office.

Will's father staked a claim, geared himself to the teeth, and shifted his daily toil from working the soil in daylight for a crop of golden wheat to plunging his pick into the earth in a black cave, in search of a golden vein. But the work was hard. The ground was a sticky clay that coated everything. Tools, clothes, and hearts. It wore away at Will's soul.

Words spoken in anger years ago seemed like no more than a few days. Will had replayed those words in his mind a hundred times a day.

"There are better ways to mine now," he'd said. "Others are getting rich, and we're just getting dirty."

His father always shook his head, offering the same wisdom every day. "When you have a claim of your own, you can mine however you like. But on my claim, you'll do it my way."

Will had had enough. That evening he'd packed up his things, taking every coin he'd saved, and headed west. Word had spread that there was gold in California, too, and he decided he'd find his share. The next day, Will had kissed his mother's tear-stained cheeks and set out for his treasure.

But of course, California was a temptress that did not yield her bosom to every young treasure-seeker. In California, he'd found a small company of miners working their way down creeks and into mountainsides. And though he'd seen the gold, held it in his hands, and crimped it between his teeth, he found that the company took the lion's share and paid him barely enough to keep him fed.

His fellow workers did share a secret or two with him. They had laughed when he told them about the black, slimy muck that kept the gold just out of reach.

"Are you brainless? The reason the mud is so sticky is that it's rich with silver. You left a place giving out handfuls of silver to come here for a few grains of gold."

Four years he had wasted because he was anxious to make a fortune. Four years working his fingers to the bone. Four years nearly starving. Four years without Kate.

And in the meantime, Henry Comstock had discovered the secret. By the time Will heard the news of the Comstock Lode, he was selling off what little he had to make the trip back home to Virginia City. He had left for gold, but he would return for silver.

After all this time, he was no closer to having the money for a homestead of his own. Without that, a life with Kaitlin Grosvenor was still just a dream.

But if his father would receive him home and allow him to work the claim, it shouldn't take long to earn enough money for a small place. That's all they needed.

He wanted to ride a little more, but Will's horse, Tiger, was weary, nearly stumbling on the flat road. He needed to camp for the night. One more day would not make a difference.

As the sun was sinking behind him, Will directed Tiger to the creek bank for a drink before setting up camp. He dropped to his knees and took a long draft as the horse refreshed himself, snorting the cold water and splashing it over his tired back.

"Now, watch yourself." Will admonished the great beast as he ducked away from the spray. "I don't wanna sleep in soaked clothes, and I don't have anything else." He freed his canteen strap from the saddle horn and shook out the last stale drops. Immersing the round tin in the creek, he captured a cupful of mountain runoff. He swished it around and poured it back out. Even in the twilight, he could see the muck in the earth-stained liquid. He repeated the process until the water came out clear, then filled the canteen with enough fresh water to keep him satisfied the rest of the way home.

Tiger whinnied and reared up without warning, and Will felt the shadow of a large owl swooping too close. "Whoa, boy. Settle. You're all right. We're safe. Settle down."

But a chill took hold, and Will didn't feel all right. Grabbing Tiger's reins, Will pulled him a little way from the water, hoping to avoid whatever wildlife might come for a midnight sip. He gathered a stack of wood and twigs for kindling, and within a half-hour had built a nice blaze.

Just as the last orange clouds turned dark purple, Will had his camp set. Tiger was tethered to an old tree where he could enjoy a rare patch of fresh grass. He stretched out over his bedroll, resting his head in the cradle of his saddle. With his canteen at one elbow and his nearly empty saddlebag at the other, he was ready to eat. He scrounged through the leather pouch blindly and found his mark.

He took the slip of yellowed paper and unfolded it with his left hand as he gripped the last strip of jerky with his right. Tearing off a mouthful, he held the paper to the firelight and read.

Dearest William, you know that I love you and that I always will. But unless our fortunes change, I fear we cannot build a home together. My father insists that I keep myself for someone with money and a name. I wish you luck in California. You will always be in my heart. Kaitlin.

He read the note again and again, as he had every night since she gave it to him. He heard her honied voice whisper the words. He saw her pushing her blonde curls back from her face. He remembered the smell of the lilac perfume she dabbed on her wrists and felt her soft pink hand on his cheek as he kissed her good-bye.

Will hadn't wanted to leave her, but it was the only way. He thought he'd never find fortune in Virginia City. And he'd never have Kate without it.

He refolded the letter and slipped it back into his bag. He folded the wax wrapper around the jerky to save one more bite for tomorrow. As he started to doze off, Tiger snorted and began stomping from side to side.

Bolting upright in his bed, Will scanned his camp, ready to fight. "What is it, boy?"

Tiger pulled at his tether and lurched away from the fire. His neigh was nervous and short, and his eyes were wide. Will listened for an intruder or an approaching animal but heard nothing. He got to his feet and peered into the night in every direction.

Deciding the firelight might be impeding his view, he took a few paces away from camp and stepped off a wider perimeter. Only stars overhead. Nothing to the north, to the west, and to the south. But to the east—beyond the horizon—an orange glow reached up into the purple-black. Will stared for several minutes, half-expecting to see the moon rise.

It took him several more anxious minutes to realize that the moon was already up and shining its bright white full face.

The young man blinked several times, almost convinced that he imagined the glow. He looked away again, turning in a full circle. But when he turned back, the glow was still there. And something more. Gray wispy fingers reached up to the moon from the glow. He watched for a few minutes more until the gray disappeared, and the orange glow dulled to a violet.

Hearing nothing but his heart pounding in his ears, Will walked back to his camp.

"Nothing out there, Tiger. Let's get some rest."

As the horse settled down, Will moved his bedroll a few inches closer to the fire. He sat down and stirred the embers, trying to build up the flames a little more. The yellow tongues licked higher into the darkness, and Will felt satisfied that it would last the night.

He propped himself against the saddle again and swiveled his head to check from one side to another. Quiet. Will squinted his eyes to see if the glow was still visible. Everything was black around him.

His thoughts drifted to his last ride home. "Of course," he murmured to himself, realizing the glow had come from the direction of Virginia City. It was just the little town shutting down for the night.

Crossing his arms over his chest to keep the chill away, Will shifted down on the blanket and propped his hat over his face. He wanted to dream. But not of swooping owls or prowling creatures. He didn't even want to dream of silver. He wanted to dream of a little white house with a garden to the side. Of a kitchen that smelled of stew and a wife with a honey-sweet voice. He wanted to dream of Kate.

CHAPTER

TWO

The numbing cold of still morning air roused Will from his sleep as the sun was just peeking over the horizon. His body was stiff and didn't want to move. He rubbed his eyes and sat up, scooping his hat from the ground beside him and resting it on the saddle horn. He looked around at his campsite. Everything looked as he had left it last night, except the fire had dwindled from a blaze to a ring of white ash with a hint of orange glow underneath.

Will started to poke at the embers, hoping to stir them back to a small flame, but he remembered he had no food save the bite of jerky, and that didn't need to be warmed. Besides, he'd be home soon, and Mama always had something saved back.

Tiger, looking especially grand silhouetted in the sunrise, seemed as anxious as Will. He stamped at the dirt and pulled against his lead.

"Hold up, boy. I have a little business to tend to," Will said, stepping to a clump of sagebrush a few paces from the camp to relieve himself.

Coming back to the rock ring around the embers, Will emptied his canteen on the ash, sending a white puff of smoke into his face. He coughed and rocked back. "I'm awake now."

Tiger whinnied and pulled again, and Will decided maybe the horse had something wrong with it. As he rounded the front of the horse to untie the tether from the tree, he saw that Tiger's mane, usually a long warm gray, was dark and soaked with blood.

Will's heart pounded in his chest. "No, Tiger! What happened to you?" he yelled, scanning the horse's head, ears, and neck for a wound. The blood was all over Tiger and quickly covered Will's arms and shirt as he searched for the injury. "I don't see where you're hurt, boy. What happened?"

The dapple gray bounced his nose on Will's shoulder and nudged the young man toward the tree.

"I'll getcha loose. You're so impatient." Will shook his head and started working on the leather strap, still trying to figure out where the blood came from.

The tether was stuck from Tiger's insistent pulling, and it took Will several minutes to get it untied. As soon as the knot was loose, Tiger bolted toward the fire ring. As he did, his rump knocked against Will, causing him to tumble back against the tree.

Will held the trunk tightly to steady himself, causing a black mass to fall from the upper branches onto Will's back. He jumped away, afraid it was a wild animal, but whatever it was landed on the ground and didn't move.

"Scared the fire outta me!" Will spit out, along with a few other choice curses. He took the stick from the fire ring and cautiously edged closer to the mass. He poked it once or twice, but it didn't move of its own volition. Another sharp jab sent it rolling into a bright beam of sunlight. At this point, Will could make out that the creature was a small gray fox, saturated in its own blood.

On closer inspection, Will could see that the fox had its throat torn open. "Poor thing." He pushed the carcass away from the camp. "I suppose that's where all this blood came from." He peered up into the branches over his head. "But how'd the dang thing get way up there?"

Tiger didn't answer. Will grabbed the lead and pulled the horse back down to the river for a quick bath. He peeled his blood-soaked shirt off and held it in the cold, rushing water, watching as the stains turned pink and then seemed to fade out of the old shirt completely. He tossed the tunic over a low branch and began hand-ladling cold water over Tiger's face, mane, and shoulder. He scrubbed at his gray hair for several minutes, spreading the pink stain over more of the protesting horse.

"Quit acting the baby," Will nagged. "I know it's cold, but it'll dry."

He saw a yucca plant just up the bank. "You hold here for a second, boy. I've got an idea." Will took his knife from the small sheath and used it to dig around the edge of the yucca until he loosened it from the dirt. He carefully kicked the plant over to bare the roots, then employed the knife again to slice away a chunk of the roots to use for soap.

Coming back to Tiger's side, he held the yellow-white root in the stream for a second, then scooped up another handful of water for Tiger's mane. With the root in one hand and water in the other, he scrubbed at Tiger's hair until it was mostly back to gray.

"See there, boy? Now you're cleaner than me."

Picking his shirt from off the tree branch, Will grabbed Tiger's strap and led him back to their campsite. He saddled the horse and stowed all his gear in place.

Will draped his still-damp shirt over the saddle and retrieved his canteen. "One more trip down to the stream, and then we'll be ready to go."

The pair ambled back to the water's edge, and Tiger drank as Will filled the tin with cold water again.

William slid into his shirt, took his seat atop Tiger, and began arguing with himself over whether to eat the last of the jerky for breakfast or save it for lunch.

"If I eat it now, then I won't have anything later." He flapped the tails of his shirt, unwilling to button the front until it had dried a little more. "I know, Tiger, and you're right," he said as if the horse was presenting the opposing argument. "But right now, I'm shivering cold. I'd likely shiver off whatever sustenance the jerky offered before the sun gets half up one side."

Tiger snorted. Will wondered if he did it on purpose, just to actually be part of the conversation.

"That's a good point." Will gave the horse a gentle kick to hurry him a bit. "Let's us make a deal, then. When the sun is straight overhead, I'll eat the last of the jerky. By then, we should be able to see the road leading up to town."

Another snort.

"Then we're agreed."

After another hour, filled with semi-one-sided conversation about what Mama might be fixing for dinner and how good a real bed was gonna feel, Will noticed a half-dozen vultures circling over something just out of sight.

They would float in high rings, and then one would swoop down, nearly to the ground, and then soar back up with the others, slipping right back into his place.

As they got closer, Will saw one dive and come back up with something clutched in his talons. Not sure what it was, Will pushed his hat back from his face to get a better look. Maybe a rabbit. Slightly bigger, it appeared. But at this distance, with the angle of the sun, Will was only guessing what the shadows might be. Maybe a raccoon. The vultures' circle dipped lower in the sky.

The bird clutching the animal took a quick dip down and then let the creature drop from its grasp and fall to the earth. Will was just close enough to see it hit and break open on impact. "Ugh!" he gasped. "I guess we know how that fox got up in that tree. I've never seen a vulture do that before."

He pulled his hat back lower on his head and did his best to ignore the sky for a while. Goosebumps rose on his arms, and he rushed to button his shirt closed. "Why am I cold? It's gotta be nearing a hundred degrees out here already."

Will knew it wasn't anywhere near the century mark, but Tiger wasn't going to argue with him, so he could say whatever he wanted.

The sun had almost reached its apex, and Will was debating again about the jerky when he spied the main road in the distance.

Giving Tiger another kick, Will clicked his tongue and leaned forward for a few minutes of running. He wanted to be sure.

The road opened wide to greet them. It led right up to Virginia City—almost home.

Will let up and brought Tiger back to a steady trot, not wanting him to be in a lather when they rode through town. Deciding the sun was plenty high enough, Will reached into his saddlebag and brought out the last remnant of jerky. He tore it in half between his teeth, not because the piece was too big for one bite, but because enjoying two bites instead of one seemed like a more substantial meal. And Mama would ask.

With the jerky gone, Will took out his canteen and sucked down a still cool swallow. He was about to release a nice long satisfied sigh when a desert whirlwind kicked up and threw a big ole handful of dirt in his open mouth.

Coughing and wheezing, Will clutched at his water source, afraid he might drop it. It took him several minutes to expel the sand from his throat and half the canteen of water to swish and spit the grit from between his teeth.

Now he'd have to conserve his water. He wished he was a little closer to the creek, but that would take him to the opposite side of the town from the homestead. It wouldn't add much time, but he'd have to ride through the middle of Virginia City on the way home. What if he saw someone he knew? What if he saw Kate?

Everything came back to her. And though Will wanted to see her more than anyone, he didn't want her to see him looking like this. Hungry, dirty, and smelling like Tiger.

"It's not that you stink, Tiger. You smell perfectly fine for a horse.

You're probably quite attractive to lady horses. I'm sure you are. But Kaitlin isn't a horse, and she certainly doesn't smell like one." Will leaned forward to scratch Tiger's ears. "And so, I propose that we go home first. I'm sure Mama will have me wash up while she's cooking dinner. We'll eat, then get a good night's sleep, and then go into town tomorrow and find Kate."

As if he could understand, the horse picked up his pace, and when they came to the trail heading east to his parents' home, Will tugged the reins, leading Tiger through the south end of town.

The trail seemed much closer to town than when he'd left. The whole city was bigger. Much bigger. Four years ago, the town had been little more than a couple dozen homes and businesses, pinwheeling from roads going north, south, and east.

Riding around the perimeter, Will could see that there were several more small roads. More buildings than he could count. People, wagons, horses—all going from here to there and back again. It was almost like being back in California.

But Virginia City didn't smell like California. It didn't smell like the Virginia City he remembered, either. He thought about the day he'd left. The town had the aroma of sawn wood, damp earth, and manure. Today it smelled like smoke.

"Somethin's not right, Tiger," Will whispered as he looked up to the curve in the trail. He gave another gentle kick, and the horse snorted but did not increase his speed.

Will didn't push the horse. Instead, he slipped a hand under his mane and patted his neck. "Let's get home, and we'll sort it all out. We're almost there."

The horse slowed a bit and snorted, pulling his head away from the town.

Young Will thought back to the Bible stories his mother had read to him over and over as a child. He was the prodigal son returning home. "While the son was still far away, his father saw him and ran to him and put a robe on his shoulders and a ring on his finger." Will wasn't sure if it was a memory or a wish. "Do you think my father will be watching for me?" he whispered. "Do you think he'll run to us?"

The sun was heading back down now, and Will was in a hurry to get home. But he should be able to see the house by now. At least the barn. But he couldn't see anything. He rode on, telling himself he didn't want to miss dinner, but that was a lie. He wasn't thinking about food or a bath or a bed anymore.

He wanted to see his folks. To feel their embraces—hear their voices. Even a scolding would sound good to his ears. But the closer he got to their place, the further away that felt.

Will looked at the crook in the road and recognized it. He was there. But there was no there. In the dimming daylight, he could see the scorched earth and the rubble where a house once stood. There was a black mound where the barn used to be and jagged wooden beans where once the windmill stood sentry.

He dropped from the saddle, and his boots sunk into black ashen mud. The odor of smoke and burnt everything hung like an invisible cloud over his parent's homestead. The whole thing was black. Burnt and black.

Choking, Will spun around to face the city. Lamplights were blinking on as the sun touched the mountaintops in the next ridge.

"No!" he heard someone yelling over and over. It took him several minutes before he realized it was his voice. Tiger wandered to a pile of rocks a few paces away, and Will followed, not knowing what else to do.

When he reached the horse's side, Will wiped the tears from his eyes. In the center of the two piles of rocks, he saw what he feared most. Two crosses—painted white and marked with names. Victor Bancroft and Mary Bancroft.

"God, no," he cried. "Not this. Not this." He choked down salty tears as he dropped to his knees in the black muck. "Oh, Mama, I came home."

CHAPTER

THREE

Will did not return to Virginia City as the conquering hero as he'd predicted four years before. He wasn't even the prodigal son he believed. He was staggering into town like a whipped dog—a slave to misfortune.

He hadn't intended to leave the homestead, but after spending almost an hour searching for anything to salvage, he gave up. The night had settled in hard, and a cool breeze rushed down the mountains, leaving Will chilled and caked in sooty mud.

With nowhere to lay his bedroll, he decided he'd try his luck in town. He walked, leading Tiger down the middle of the street. He didn't want to soil his saddle with the black muck.

In utter bewilderment, Will found himself amidst rows of shops and houses that didn't exist when he'd left. To say the city had boomed was an understatement. He'd seen prospectors blow the sides off mountains, and that seemed like nothing compared to what had happened to this town.

The glow from the street lanterns made his way easy, and he noticed his reflection in a shop window. He resembled a black ghost, and the image sent a shudder down his spine. As he crossed an intersection, he finally saw a porch he recognized.

The little house had once been on the fringe of the settlement, but now it was fully engulfed in the city. The house was painted pale yellow with white gingerbread trim and white turned porch posts. He had spent hours on the blue wooden swing, holding hands with his fair Kate.

He froze in place, wondering what to do. He had nowhere to go. He had no home, no money, and no one expected him. He thought he'd go to the little chapel at the end of the road and beg the preacher for a place to sleep. But at this time of night, would there be anyone there to beg?

Still unsure where to go, he found his legs walking automatically to the yellow house. He stood at the gate for several minutes before he gathered the courage to open it. Still, he didn't go through.

"What am I doing, Tiger? Even if she wanted to see me, I don't want her to see me like this."

Tiger stamped at the ground and began chewing at a clump of grass at the base of the gatepost.

"But what choice do I have?" Will flipped the leather lead round the fence and drew a deep breath. He walked slowly up the stone path, up the steps to the porch, and rapped on the door, leaving muddy marks from his filthy knuckles.

A minute later, a middle-aged man opened the door and stared long and hard at Will. Will looked over the man's shoulder, seeing a woman in an apron, setting food on a table surrounded by five or six children. Will's stomach growled loudly.

"What can I do for you?" the man asked with a hint of irritation in his voice.

Will's voice scratched and stuttered. "I—I wanted to talk to Miss Grosvenor for a moment, if I may."

"What?" the man answered. "Oh, Grosvenor, you say?"

Will nodded. "Yes, sir. But just for a minute."

The man shook his head. "No, the Grosvenors are gone. We

bought the place three years ago. Eli Grosvenor died, and his missus took the children back east to live with her sister. I guess you've been gone a bit. Things have changed around here."

"I guess so. Thank you, sir." Will's heart broke all over again.

The man shut the door, and Will turned back to face Tiger, who was still munching at the grass. With each step away from the yellow house, Will felt another stab.

No family, no home, no Kate. Why had he come back? No, that wasn't the right question. Why had he left in the first place?

His stupid pride. What was it the preacher used to say? Pride goes before a fall. *Yes, it does*, Will thought. *And I have fallen hard.*

He loosened Tiger's lead and headed back toward the town's center. He could hear music from just ahead, coming from a brightly lit building. As he got closer, he saw the shingled sign hanging at the canopied walk. *The Palace Saloon.*

Will thought for a second of going inside but then realized they'd most likely throw him right back out again. He didn't have money for a shot of whiskey, certainly not enough to buy into a hand of poker.

He walked on, hoping for an idea to come. Another block, and he was standing in front of the Sheriff's office, with only the church and a few houses beyond. He looked at Tiger and shrugged. "I s'pose we'll see if maybe we can camp out behind the church."

"What's your business here?" a voice called out.

Looking around him, Will saw nobody. "Hello?" he answered.

"I said, what's your business here in Virginia City? If you're a drifter, you best keep on drifting. I don't need no troublemakers. No more than we got already." The voice was attached to a broad-shouldered man with dark hair, dark eyes, and a glistening silver star on his chest. He was stepping out of the shadows of the sheriff's office.

"No trouble, sheriff," Will said, holding his hands out, palms up. "I used to live here and just came back to town." Will eyed the man carefully. He was not Sheriff Manchin. This was someone else. "Maybe you can help me."

"That's why I'm here, son." The man strode out to the road to give Will a going-over. "Why don't we start with your name."

Nodding, Will stammered, "Yes, sir. My name is William Bancroft. My parents are, I mean were Victor and Mary Bancroft. I've been away for a few years, and I just came back today. Their place is —" his voice broke off.

The sheriff squeezed his eyes shut as he inhaled and then blew out a curse and kicked at the ground. "That's," he caught his breath before continuing. "That's some tough luck, kid. I'm sorry. If we'd known you were coming back—if we'd known you were on your way," he said and then paused.

"You'd have what?" Will asked. His tone was strained. "What are you talking about? What happened?"

"Why don't you come inside for a minute and we can talk. Tie your horse up and come in and sit. You look like hell."

William tied Tiger to the hitching post and followed the sheriff into his office. The man directed Will to a chair opposite his desk and poured out two short glasses of liquor. He pushed one to Will and took the other in his right hand.

"Sheriff," Will began.

"Gregory," the man said. "I'm Sheriff Gregory." He took a sip and dipped his chin toward Will.

"Sheriff Gregory, can you just tell me what happened to my parents? And what did you mean when you said, 'if we'd known you were coming.'" Will looked at the glass but didn't pick it up.

"Yes, of course." Gregory stared at William for a second as if he was trying to guess his weight. "Yesterday, about mid-morning, we saw a wildfire—just a small one—east of town. Out beyond your folk's place. The firehouse was called out, but by the time the water truck had got out there, the blaze had just about burnt itself out." He took another sip and again nodded to Will's glass.

Will only stared back.

"So, the wind was strange, as you might have noticed on your travels. Hot, with a fury from the east. Not the typical current that comes over the mountain, and not the cool breeze you'd expect coming up the mountain, either. No, this was whipping hot. And I guess that first fire never got all the way smothered out because just as the sun was going down, the fire started up again, this time closer to town. It took out your father's old fields. Of course, they were parched dry, not being tended to these last several years."

Gregory's words painted a vivid, horrific image in Will's mind as he imagined the wildfire lapping at his mother's garden and at his father's barn. At the house, the windmill, the fencing. Leaving nothing but the blackened bones of the homestead Will had left just an hour earlier.

"By the time the water truck got out there, the house was a loss. Everything was in flames. The whole town turned out to help—a few good citizens got some pretty bad burns. They were able to stop the fire from reaching into Virginia City. But I'm sorry to say your parents couldn't be saved." He tilted his head back and poured the rest of his drink down his throat. He leaned forward over his desk, shifting his stare from Will to the untouched glass and back. "And what I meant before," he added.

Now Will leaned toward him a fraction of an inch.

"If we'd have known you were on your way into town, we wouldn't have buried them so quickly. We'd have let you have a say in their arrangements."

Will squinted his eyes, only half-satisfied by his explanation. "But why weren't they at least buried in the churchyard. I'd have expected at least that."

Sheriff Gregory almost laughed. "You have been gone for a while, haven't you, son? Your parents haven't attended services in a few years now. Your father had it out with the preacher and got your whole family excommunicated, or whatever they call it."

At this, Will dropped back in his chair, slumping his shoulders. He was worse off than a whipped dog. He was a whipped, damned-to-hell dog.

"I hate to ask, son, but where do you intend to spend the night?"

Gregory leveled his dark eyes at Will. "I expect you'll probably be headed back from wherever you came pretty soon, being as there's nothing much left for you here."

Grabbing the glass from the desk, Will swallowed the whiskey down in one fiery gulp. It burned all the way down to his empty stomach. He started to answer, but the drink sent a gasp and a cough out first. When he'd regained his voice, he continued. "I was on my way to the church to beg for a place to sleep, but I suppose that's not an option now."

"I wouldn't if I were you."

Releasing a long sigh, Will shrugged. "Then can you direct me to somewhere I might find a bed for a night or two? At least until I can figure what to do next."

"How much money you got?"

Will dropped his head to his chest. "Nothing right now. But I can work it off. I'm strong."

Gregory exhaled through gritted teeth, making a hissing sound. "I can't present you to anyone looking like you do now. You look like a drowned street rat." He twitched his thick black mustache from side to side. "I'll tell you what. I'll get you a basin of water and a towel, and I'll let you have a cot here tonight. It's not much, but it won't cost you anything. I can even have a girl bring you over something to eat—you look like you haven't eaten in a month."

"I feel like it."

"Then tomorrow morning, we'll talk about your situation. Whether you want to stay here and work or head out for greener pastures. I can probably scrounge up some clothes for you as well, at least until we see if these come clean. How does that sound?" Gregory's smile spread wide under his whiskers.

Will squinted again. "It sounds a little too good to be true. What will I owe you?"

"Oh, you don't worry about that for now. Maybe I'll have you sweep up the place or do some mending on the roof. Such as that. Sound fair?" Gregory nodded as if he was trying to persuade Will to do the same. "And just for good measure, I'll have my man come and take your horse to the livery on me. He's a fine horse—looks as though he's eaten better than you. My man will make sure he's fed good and brushed down real nice. I'll have him check his shoes, too."

"Tiger deserves that, after what he's been through this last month." Will didn't want to hem himself in, but his horse needed attention. He couldn't see any other way to get it. "I guess that sounds good. Well, it's right generous of you. Thank you, Sheriff."

The lawman stood and gestured to the door at the back of the office. "Well, before you get too excited, I gotta set you up in your room, and it's none too fancy. The only empty bed I got is the one back here." He pulled a key from his pocket and turned it in the latch.

When the door swung open, Will peered into the small room, lit only by the lanterns outside the high window. As his eyes adjusted, he saw that he was looking into the jail cells, and on the far wall behind the rows of heavy bars, he saw the figure of a man sleeping on a cot.

Will followed Gregory into the room and watched as the sheriff lit a lantern beside the door. "You have a roommate, but you do get your own cell and your own bed."

Stepping into the little barred room, Will turned quickly to ask, "Are you going to lock me in?"

Gregory shook his head and dropped the key back into his pocket. "I don't think that's necessary, so long as you don't leave. If any of my deputies see someone other than me leaving the office, they'll most likely shoot you." He exhaled loudly. "So, I would advise against that."

Looking around the cell, Will realized that it was as good as he required for the night. The man in the other cell was snoring softly, but not any louder than Tiger most nights. "I should get my saddlebag and bedroll."

Sheriff Gregory held up his hands to stop him. "Don't you worry about that. I'll take care of that. Now you stay here and peel yourself out of those clothes. I'll bring back everything you'll need in twenty minutes. And don't you go running off, you hear me? They will shoot you."

"Where would I go without my clothes?" Will answered.

Gregory left the door to the cell opened wide but closed and locked the door to his office. Will dropped to the edge of the cot and wrestled one boot off and then the other. He tucked them under the end of the cot and started pulling at his shirt buttons.

The front of his shirt was so caked with dried ash that he could barely force the buttons through the holes. Even in the lamplight, he could see that the black had stained through his shirt to his chest. "What a mess," he whispered as he set to work on his trousers. The dark stains had soaked through to his drawers. "Ugh, I'll wait 'til he gets back. I ain't gonna sit here buck-naked."

"Thank God for small favors," a voice said.

Will spun around to see the man in the cot was now sitting up and rubbing his eyes. "What did you say?" his voice was defensive.

"I said that nobody on this earth wants to see you naked, Will Bancroft. Least of all me." The man stood and walked the two and a half steps to the bars that separated their cells.

As the man came closer to the lantern, Will could see his square bronzed face and crooked smile. He recognized the scar that cut his right eyebrow in two. It was his friend from childhood, Joseph Dark Water, from the nearby Shoshone settlement.

"Joseph, what are you doing in here?" Will asked, grateful to see his friend again.

"I could ask you the same question." Joseph reached through the bars and clasped Will's wrists. "I never thought I would see you again, my friend. I am sorry for your folks, Will."

"You heard what happened?"

Joseph dropped his head in a respectful nod. "Please, Will, whatever the sheriff or anyone else tells you, you have to believe me. I had nothing to do with your parent's deaths."

CHAPTER

FOUR

"And two deputies grabbed me and tossed me in here. They're saying I started the fire. Suggesting I did it on purpose." Joseph was sitting on the edge of his cot, his elbows propped on his knees. "I wasn't anywhere close to where the wildfire started. I only went to help put it out." Joseph gestured to his hair and face. "When you look like me, you're always guilty of something, I guess."

Will released an awkward laugh. "I have no stones to cast, friend."

"I am truly sorry about your parents, Will. I can tell you that the whole city was out there, trying to stop the fire."

"I should have been there for them." As Will finished his statement, the men heard sounds coming from the front room.

Joseph held a finger to his lips and then rolled back onto his cot as if he was sleeping again.

Jumping to his feet, Will moved to the opening of his cell, waiting for the adjacent door to swing clear. He could hear the key turn in the lock and watched as a stripe of light shone from the front office into the dimmer jail room. An older woman carrying a washbasin and pitcher timidly entered the room, followed closely by Gregory, carrying a small tray of food.

"Thank you, Carol Ann, that's all we'll need for tonight." Gregory waited for the woman to set the bowl onto the table by the lantern and hand the towel she had on her arm to Will. She dipped her round frame into an almost-curtsy and then hurried from the room. Gregory set the tray of food on the opposite corner of the table from the rest.

"I'm awfully grateful, Sheriff. And I'll get you repaid just as soon as I'm able." Will realized that he was still wearing only his mud-stained underwear and crossed his hands low to convey a sense of modesty.

Gregory chortled and went back to his office for a moment. "I almost forgot," he said, tossing a bundle across the room. "Don't want you to catch your death."

Will caught the clothes and carefully placed them on his cot. "Again, thanks."

"They may be a might big on you, but you look like a man who can make do." The lawman paused for a second as another humming snore rose from Joseph's bed. "Sorry about that, but you'll only be here for the night. We'll get you a better situation tomorrow."

"Don't worry about me, Sheriff. My horse snores louder than that."

The sheriff laughed again and then turned his expression serious. "Well, Mr. Bancroft, I'm glad you mentioned your horse. He's a fine ride. You've taken good care of him."

"Yes, sir. Tiger's taken good care of me." Will started to wonder where this conversation was going.

"Tiger, huh?" Gregory shrugged. "Well, the boy at the livery said the horse looked a little rough and could use a few days of rest and care. That'll give you plenty of time to earn a little to cover whatever expenses you may tally and give you a bit of travel money to boot."

Will took a step forward and paused. "I don't want to sound—" he paused again. "I am in your debt. And I appreciate the concern for

Tiger." He took another breath, not wanting to show his worry. "Would I be able to check in on him tomorrow morning? I'm not distrustful, but my horse and I haven't been apart since I was a kid. And he gets nervous."

Nodding, Gregory shoved his hands into his pockets. "Won't be a problem at all. Now, go on and get your drawers changed and fill your belly. We'll find you a place to be proud of in the morning." He dipped his chin toward the food. "And Carol Ann's cooking ain't the best in town, but I figured you'd like it more than mine."

"Thank you, sir," Will replied. "It's better than fine, sir."

Sheriff Gregory touched his finger to the brim of his hat in a salute and turned back out of the room, closing the door behind him.

Will heard the latch click as Joseph rolled back over with a finger over his mouth. "Don't make too much noise until we know he's gone," Joseph whispered.

Opening the bundle of clothes, Will looked each piece over. Shirt, trousers, drawers, socks, bandana, and a string tie. He tossed a glance at the plate of stew. "Maybe I should eat it while it's hot."

Joseph shook his head. Still keeping his voice low, he said, "If Carol Ann made it, being cold won't make it any worse than it is now. Wash up and put some clothes on."

Will laughed and positioned himself beside the basin. He pulled his underwear off and tossed them on top of the heap of his soiled clothing. He half-filled the bowl and dipped a corner of the towel in the clean water. He leaned over the bowl and washed his hair, face, and neck, scrubbing away the soot and ash as he went.

As his mother had taught him, he dipped, scrubbed, and rinsed. He started behind his ears and was almost to his knees before the water was dark gray. By then, the towel was nearly soaked through, and he used it to scrape off the black from his calves and feet. Satisfied, he pulled on his fresh linens, leaving off his tie, bandana, pants, and socks for the night.

He leaned close to the plate to sniff at the stew. Smelling nothing, he leaned a little closer. "Joseph, I think my sniffer is busted. I can't tell one way or another what kind of meat this is."

His friend clicked his tongue. "Sad to say, taking a bite won't help you, either."

"You want any?" Will offered.

"No." Joseph leaned back on the cot. "But I think it will be fun to watch you try it."

"Ah, hush," Will said, shaking his head. "It can't be that bad." He scooped up a fat spoonful and plunged the meat and bean concoction into his mouth. There was almost no flavor at all. In fact, Will thought that maybe some of the ash water from his bath had splashed into the mixture. The meat resisted Will's chewing, and the beans became stringy as Will's teeth munched down hard. "It is that bad."

"I warned you."

Shaking off the non-flavor, Will took another bite. However terrible it was, his stomach still growled, and his hands were shaking from lack of nourishment. With the third bite, Will scooped more sauce and less meat, hoping for a little more taste. The broth was mealy, and his stomach lurched with the combination of unappetizing textures. He swallowed as quickly as he could and took a drink straight from the water pitcher.

"Ugh, even the water tastes like dirt." He wiped his mouth with the back of his hand. "This is not the town I left four years ago."

Joseph grimaced. "Glad you finally noticed. Virginia City is a den of iniquity, as the preacher chants every Sunday."

"How would you know? You don't go to church." Will scoffed at his friend.

"That's how loud the man chants. You can hear him yell all the way out to the Shoshone settlement if the wind is from the right direction." Joseph looked down at his hands. "Things are different, though." He stretched back out on his cot and stared at the ceiling. "I once could come and go as I pleased. See my friends, drink a little, gamble a bit." He looked as though he was remembering a happier time. "Maybe win enough to buy something nice at the general store."

"And you can't do those things anymore?"

"No, I can't. These days, I come into town, and almost immediately, I'm picked up and brought here. A day or two later, my uncle comes in, pays a fine, and takes me back home. At least I have that. The sheriff is still scared of my uncle." Joseph sighed. "But if anything were to happen to him, I'd be hanging in the square by noon."

"But if you're not doing anything wrong?" Will dropped his spoon into the half-eaten stew. "What can they charge you with?"

"I'm a red man, Will. My people raid and slaughter for fun. Didn't they teach you that in your little white schoolhouse?" Joseph's tone was bitter and sarcastic.

"Come on, man. I know you. I know your uncle—shoot, I know your whole family. What? We've been friends since we were kids. Since that first time you caught me shooting rabbits out in the field behind your father's wagon. I thought I was dead for sure."

"See?" Joseph sat up and stared at Will. "Your first thought was that I would hurt you."

"And instead, you taught me the right way to shoot," Will said.

"You were doing it all wrong. It's a wonder you didn't break your shoulder, holding your gun like that." Joseph dropped back on his bed. "Whatever happened to that rifle? It was a good one."

"Had to sell it to pay for the last leg of my trip to California. Everything is more expensive than you expect." Will took another drink of water and spit it into the basin. Leaning over the lantern, he cupped his hand at the chimney and puffed the light out.

He leaned back on his cot and stretched out until his feet hung over the edge. He closed his eyes and let a few deep breaths in and out as his eyes adjusted to the dark blue of the night, consuming the once-lit room.

"Tomorrow, before you do anything else, you need to check on your horse and tell him good-bye," Joseph whispered.

"Good-bye?"

"The sheriff is never going to let you have him back—not like he says." Joseph's voice sounded tired. "But I guess you know this. You're a smart man."

Will's stomach tightened into a knot. Part of him did know this, but he didn't want to believe it. He wouldn't. "What do you mean?"

Joseph turned to face the wall again. "Gregory had you under his thumb from the moment you met him. He brought you inside, explained about the fire. He took good care of your horse, got you food, a bath, and some clothes."

"And I'm gonna pay him back for all that." Will knew he was good for it. A few days of work somewhere—anywhere—and he'd be square. "Before I do anything else, I'll have Tiger back."

"Back where?" Joseph asked. "You don't have a home in Virginia City anymore. They saw to that."

Will sat up straight in his bed and faced Joseph, well, his back. His tone was stern. "Who saw to that? What do you know about the fire?" Will's voice cracked. "You said you didn't start it, but you act like you know who did. What's going on, Joseph?"

Joseph snored slowly.

"Stop that right now," Will barked. "You said you were in jail for starting the fire, but Sheriff Gregory said it was just a brush fire that got out of control. Don't you think he'd have told me you did it if he believed that?"

Like a ghost rising from a grave, Joseph sat back up in his bed, the moonlight turning him into a glowing silhouette. "He knows it isn't true. But he needs someone to blame."

Will could hear Joseph's voice, but in the shadows, he couldn't see his lips moving. A shudder streaked down his back.

"That's how the town works now. Bad people do bad things, and someone has to pay. But never the bad people. They're the ones in control. It has to be someone else. I'm an easy scapegoat. But I'm not always available. So sometimes it's good folk who pay. Enough that the good ones stay quiet. Enough that everyone is afraid that they'll be next."

Fear crept up Will's spine like a spider. "Then there's no reason for me to stay here. I don't know where I'll go, but I don't have ties here anymore. I'll go. As soon as I get paid up and get Tiger back, I'll just go."

Joseph nodded and lay back down. "I wish you luck. But I fear that Gregory will set you up with a room and a job, and you'll have a choice to make. Commit to him long-term or be the next scapegoat."

"No. I'll just work until I have Tiger back." Will exhaled again, trying to throw off the nagging at his brain. He stretched out, his muscles aching and twitching.

"Then he'll find something else to hold over you. If it's not Tiger, it will be something else. Or someone else." He sighed, and his voice softened as if he was falling asleep. "There's always something."

Will rolled away from his friend and grunted. The bath had not made him clean. The food had not filled his belly. The bed did not comfort him. He had hoped for rest. But sleep never came.

CHAPTER

FIVE

The jail room door slammed open with a bang, sending Will to his feet. Joseph lazily rolled over to face the deputy who had done the slamming.

The young man with the badge lunged forward to close Will's cell door that was still standing wide open. "Blast if I knew how you got that open!"

"Slow down, Gil. He's not in here for breaking the law. Sheriff Gregory gave him a bed for the night." Joseph's tone was low, and his words rolled out slowly. "I'm the only criminal in here today."

Gil chuffed. "We'll see about that. Sheriff will be here shortly."

"Is my uncle here, yet?" Joseph barely paused for a breath.

"One of these days, Dark Water." Gil growled as he turned the key in the iron lock. "Your uncle won't be here to get you out. Then where will you be?"

Joseph shrugged. "I guess then I'll just be in here with you." Joseph turned to face Will. "Take care of yourself, stranger. Stay out of trouble."

"You, too," Will replied. "Maybe I'll see you around."

"Doubt it," Joseph muttered under his breath. "I don't plan on being around."

Will watched the deputy usher Joseph into the office, closing the jail door again and locking it. "I gotta get some clothes on," he whispered to himself. He hurried to dress and prepare for whatever the day would bring.

He'd spent all night wallowing in the what-ifs, and he had no more clarity than he did when he first rode into town. Was Joseph right about the sheriff? About the town? He'd played through every word he exchanged with Gregory. Nothing sounded wrong or out of place.

But that feeling he had in his gut—that came even before he'd talked to Joseph. The sheriff was too accommodating. Too eager to help. He did show concern for Tiger, but that could have been because he was planning to take him.

His stomach was in knots again, and his head ached from all the worrying. Sitting on the edge of the cot, he waited for the door to open again. He heard voices outside the door. Chairs scraping the floor. Another door opening and then closing again. Keys jingled. More voices. The slam of a door and then silence.

"I guess somebody forgot I was here." He got up again and paced the floor, listening to his stomach growl again. For a split second he considered trying last night's stew, but when he looked in the bowl, his stomach lurched. "Maybe not."

Pacing back and forth did nothing but make him tired, so he went back to the cot. He sat for several minutes, his gaze boring a hole into the door. His eyelids grew heavy, and he let his back rest against the wall. "Jus' for a moment."

When he finally awoke, the sun was high in the sky, and the cell had warmed considerably. He felt a bead of perspiration forming at his hairline. Stretching his arms out to his side, he became aware of noises from the other room. He decided not to wait to be rediscovered.

Walking to the door, he tapped and listened. "Hello? Is someone there?" He listened again and heard footfalls approaching. Stepping back, he released a sigh of relief when the door swung open.

"Sorry about the wait, son." Gregory chomped on a stub of a cigar wedged into the far-left side of his mouth. "I did find you a room, but I had to negotiate to find something that would leave some silver in your pocket. I figured you needed a little extra sleep anyway."

"I did. Thank you, sir," Will heard himself saying. Joseph would have sneered at his manners. But his friend had left him there, so what did his opinion matter anyway? "And thank you for finding me a room."

"Got you a good-paying job too. Of course, it's temporary, but it will last you until you're ready to head out to wherever you're going." Gregory led him out of the cell and into the main office. "Leave everything in there but your new duds. Carol Ann will come to pick it up after the lunch rush. She'll wash up your clothes, too. She's a good woman, Bancroft."

"It was kind of her to make me dinner," Will said, trying hard to say something polite about the meal. He hoped Gregory didn't ask how it tasted. "If you don't mind me asking, can we stop by the livery to see my horse? I just want to let him know that I'm okay. Sometimes he gets nervous without me, and—well, I'm sure you know what a mess a nervous horse can make."

Gregory laughed. "Ain't that the truth." He didn't answer Will's question. "First thing, I'm gonna take you to see a man at the Enterprise. You're going to work as a messenger of sorts—doing odd jobs. How does that suit you?"

"I suppose that's fine. But won't I need my horse for that?" He hoped that might serve as a hint about visiting Tiger. It didn't seem to work.

"You won't for starting off. The Enterprise is a local paper. You'll mostly be running stories from one person to another. They may have you truck papers out to be sold. Minor things like that." Gregory led Will out to the street and gestured toward the center of town.

The bright sunlight burned Will's eyes. The city streets were quiet now. Citizens hurried from one place to another, but there was no music or raucous voices from last night. Virginia City was much bigger now than when he'd left, but the overall appearance in the daylight seemed much closer to his memories.

As they walked, Will studied the shingles hanging over the storefronts. A tailor here, a millinery there. The General Store was still in place, though the sign had changed. Will tried to remember if the owner's name had changed or if it was just the fancy sign.

Minutes later, the men walked up the steps and through the doors of the Territorial Enterprise. As they were going in, another man was coming out.

"Afternoon, gentlemen," he said, tipping his chin in respect. The man's chin was narrow, and it appeared even more so because it competed with a thick dark mustache and an even thicker head of wild dark hair. The whole face was accented with the bushiest dark brows Will had ever seen on a man who was still obviously in his twenties.

"Afternoon," Will answered with a nod.

Entering the front office, Gregory gestured to a door behind a long counter. "Right back here."

Will followed, nodding to an older man working behind the counter and a young boy stacking folded newspapers onto a small cart.

The boy was chanting, "Out with the old and in with the new," as if it was entirely part of the task.

"Good day, friends." A plump man with bright red cheeks stood up when Will and Gregory entered. "Ah, yes," gesturing to Will, "I think he'll be quite suitable for the job. We have plenty of children to sell the papers, but it's often quite a chore for them to carry them to their stations and keep them stocked. We need muscle for that. A growing city needs its voice. We at the Enterprise want to bring it to the people."

The man sounded almost like a barker at a traveling carnival or maybe a politician. Will had heard both in the time he'd spent in California. Jovial men speaking sweet persuasions for the opportunity to part a man from his dollar. The good ones made a sap believe it was his own idea. Will suspected this man was good.

Holding out a pink hand with sausage fingers toward Will, the man said, "I'm Carson Jacobs. I have a feeling we're going to get along fine, son."

Will shook his hand. "William Bancroft. Good to know you, sir."

"Shall we get you started then?" Jacobs asked, looking at Gregory with a caricature of a smile.

The sheriff held up a halting hand. "Let me get some food into the boy. He hasn't had anything to eat today. And I need to take him to get set up in his new room."

"Right!" Jacobs plopped back into his chair. "Bring him around once he's settled, and I'll put him to work."

Will nodded. "Thank you, sir." He shuffled back into the front room, where the boy continued his chant.

The men stepped outside to face the front of a tall red brick building with a broad balcony spanning the front and white plaster pediments over the second-story windows.

"Here we are at your new home." Gregory motioned to the window at the far-left side of the balcony. "That's yours for the time being." He made a sweeping motion to the entrance doors. "Let's get you your key."

Will took a deep nervous breath as he stepped inside. Though the room was almost empty, the lingering aroma of cigar smoke, wood polish, and various liquors hung heavy in the air. He became over-aware of the sound of his boots on the wood planks of the floor. Looking down, he realized that his boots were still stained with the black mud.

"Is there somewhere I can find some polish for my boots?" he asked Gregory.

The lawman looked at the dirt. "I have just the solution." He led Will to an alcove at the foot of the stairway, where a man with a short red beard stood, writing on a notepad. "Where's the girl?" Gregory asked.

"Up making beds and cleaning up for tonight."

"This is Bancroft." Gregory hitched his thumb over Will's chest. "I've set him up in thirteen, but he needs a meal and to have his boots polished."

Redbeard nodded without looking up. "Leave your boots here with me, and you can eat through there. When you're done, the boots will be waiting for you. Thirteen, eh?"

"Yes."

"I'll add it to the bill."

Gregory gestured to a short bench against the wall. "Take 'em off, son. We'll pick them back up soon enough."

Will sat and pulled at one heel and then the next, shaking the boots loose and then sliding them in place at the end of the bench. "Feels wrong to be out where folks can see me in my stocking feet."

The sheriff ushered him through a set of double doors to a narrow table against the far wall. "Plenty of things feel wrong at first, and then turn out to be just fine. Especially in this place."

Pulling out a chair, Will sat, and Gregory took his place across from him. Will squinted as his gaze roamed the small dining room. The saloon space had been open and expansive, but this room seemed like an afterthought. "Not many folks come here for lunch?"

"This is more of a sundown place," Gregory explained. "They come here for a good time. You'll see tonight."

Carol Ann bustled out with two plates of pan-fried meat and potatoes and set the plates in front of the men. "Eat up," she chirped and rushed back to the kitchen.

Will stared at the food, filled with trepidation. He braced himself for another stomach-churning meal. But then the smell of sweet onions and seasoned beef tickled his nose. "This smells wonderful." Will's voice was filled with astonishment.

"That's because it's not Carol Ann's cooking." Gregory kept his voice low. "This will keep you full for the day."

"And when we're done with lunch, can we take a moment at the livery? I really do want to check on Tiger." Will sliced off a bite of meat and skewered it alongside a cube of potato. The flavor of the broth, salt, and onion that saturated the meat dish made his stomach sing hallelujah. He finally felt comfortable for the first time since coming back to town.

"First, you need to see your accommodations. I think you'll like the room really well." Gregory spoke as he chewed. "Everything you need."

Both men ate quickly, and, as Redbeard had said, Will's boots were shining clean and waiting for him at the bench. He pulled them back on and followed as Gregory led him up the stairs and through the turning hallways to the door marked "13."

Gregory slipped a tasseled key into the lock and opened the door to the sunlight-flooded room. It wasn't large, but the bed was bigger than anything he'd ever slept on before, covered with a dark blue coverlet and a quilt at the foot. Four pillows rested against the brass headboard, and on the far side of the bed stood a night table with a lamp. Across from the bed was a dresser with a small oval mirror on the wall. The top drawer was half-open, and Will saw that his filthy clothes from yesterday were clean and folded inside.

"Everything you need," Gregory repeated.

A narrow wooden chair sat in front of the long window leading to the balcony. Will crossed the room to look out. "Even a view of the mountains from here."

"It's a good room." Gregory nodded and pointed to under the chair. "A boot jack for you here." He waved his hand to the little commode stand behind the door. "A bowl and pitcher filled with fresh water every afternoon. Your pot down below." He let the door almost close. "And a hook for your hat."

Will had never expected anything so grand. In fact, he thought, the jail cell was much more like his typical accommodations than this room. "And I can afford this with the job at the paper?"

The sheriff looked down at his feet and back up to Will. "Kid, I have a feeling about you. I think you're about to come into a full-fledged lucky streak. I'm fronting you a little, putting up a stake for you at the poker tables here at the Palace. I think you're going to do right fine—enough to pay me back and come out ahead—ahead on this room and everything."

Will's face flushed red. "I never have won much at the tables. Maybe I should try and find something a little simpler. This is nice, and don't think I'm ungrateful, but I'd hate to let you down, Sheriff, after all you've done for me.

"Nonsense." Gregory's voice was sharp. "I feel this in my gut. And my gut is never wrong, boy."

Shaking his head, Will answered. "No, I didn't mean to insult you. I just don't want to let you down."

"Bancroft, know this," he said. Draping his arm over Will's shoulders and leading him back out the door. "Whatever happens, you will not let me down." He handed the key to Will, and they walked back to the street.

The church bell chimed once, and Gregory gestured to the Territorial Enterprise office. "I didn't mean to keep you so long, but now I'm late getting you to your new job. How 'bout I swing by after you're done, and I'll take you to the livery to see your horse. And tonight, I'll introduce you to folks and even buy your first drink at the Palace."

Will felt like a sheep being herded from one place to another. Back at the entrance to the newspaper door, he turned to Gregory. "When I'm done," he started to ask.

The sheriff interrupted. "I'll be waiting for you right here. You don't need to worry about a thing."

CHAPTER

SIX

Will had barely cleared the door when Jacobs burst through the back entrance, "Bancroft, young man, I am delighted to have you with us. Now follow me, and I'll get you situated. Oh, the lads will be thrilled to have you here."

On the heels of the portly man, Will found himself in a long narrow room and weaved himself through a series of desks staffed with men clicking away at little black typewriters, reading stacks of papers, and one man staring at the ceiling while sharpening his pencil with a knife. Will realized it was the man with bushy eyebrows and smiled when the man turned his gaze down and toward him.

"Sam, get to work!" Jacobs snapped.

Hurrying his pace to keep up, Will passed Sam's desk and pursued Jacobs to a room in the back of the building. On one side was a huge contraption that reminded Will of a hay-baler. Blank paper went in, and printed paper came out. Two men stood on either side, working to keep gears turning.

The other side was a big empty area of floor space. In between were two long narrow tables, where several older boys were folding and stacking the newly printed papers. The boy at the end was whipping twine around the stacks at a lightning pace.

The boys at the table jumped to attention when Jacob's stopped in front of them. "Men, you're doing a fine job. And I'd like to introduce you to Bill Bancroft."

"Will, sir," Will corrected when Jacob's paused for a breath.

"What was that?" Jacobs asked, turning his whole round body to face him.

"My name is Will Bancroft."

"That's what I said." Jacobs continued. "Bancroft here will be taking your bundles and loading them onto the trucks. You won't have to stop anymore to do that. Now, back to work, all of you."

Will turned back to face Jacobs, waiting to be told what to do. "Yes, sir."

The man waved his hand. "Well, get started." He flipped the palm of his hand up and to the back door. Against the wall by the door were a dozen small flat-bed wagons. "The hand trucks are there. Load six bundles to a truck and wheel them to the door. And a few of my carriers have their own wagons and carts. Be ready to load them up, too."

Nodding, Will shifted toward the carts.

"Wait," Jacobs said. "When you're done with that, you'll load the rest of the papers into the pull cart out back. Then you'll drive them out to the stations that have run out. Jack, here," pointing to the boy with the twine, "will explain the route."

"Yes, sir." Will waited for more instructions.

"Now, get going." Jacobs waved him away and rushed back through the door toward the writers. "Sam, back to work," his voice called out before the door slammed closed.

Will nodded toward the boys, and when none of them looked his way, he went to retrieve the carts. He found that each one had a handle at one end and a hook at the other. "Like mining carts," he whispered to himself.

He linked them together and pulled them in a train to line up in front of the tables. Starting at the far end, he began shifting the bundles from the table to the cart. Stacking two bundles high and three across. Once he'd got them loaded, he pulled from the last cart, moving them to the back door.

Before he had them in place, each boy had another bundle ready. He moved them, two bundles at a time, into stacks against the wall, close to the door where they could be easily picked up.

After the press was shut down and quiet, the boys still had bundles to fold. Jack was the first to finish and began helping Will stack as he described the delivery route to the paper stations. As each of the other boys finished their work, they pulled off their heavy black aprons and lined up at a water basin to wash their hands.

"That was a nice trick with the carts," Jack said. "We didn't know you could link them together. It made for short work."

"When I saw the hooks, I thought of mining cars." Will looked at the black ink covering his hands and arms.

"You've worked in the mines?" Jack asked.

"Yes, here when I was about your age," Will explained. "And in California for the last few years."

Jack's voice quickened, and his eyes widened. "Did you strike gold? Or silver? Where in California were you?"

Will laughed as they finished their last stack. "All over. And I got a little gold and a little silver. Not enough to get rich off of, but enough to know what it must be like."

"I'm going to stake a claim in a few years. Mother says I'm too young, and it's too dangerous, but soon I'll be on my own, and I'll head to California." Jack skipped after Will as they both headed to the washbasin. "Where do you recommend I go?"

Will shook his head. "You wanna know where I recommend? I recommend you stay here and take care of your mother. She's going to need you someday. If you're in California, you won't know about it until it's too late."

"Ugh, you sound like everyone else around here. Well, not everyone, but you sound like my mother."

Scrubbing the ink off his hands, Will sighed, regretting that he had waited so long to come back. He leveled his gaze at Jack. "She's a wise woman."

Will stepped away from the basin to dry his hands on a towel, and Jack snapped back to his side.

"You said you worked in a mine here. Which claim?" Jack shook his hands to dry them.

"I worked my father's claim."

"Your father has a mine here?"

"No. Not anymore." Will swallowed hard. He didn't want to talk about any of this.

Jack continued, still excited. "He sold it?"

Will exhaled, running out of patience. "No. He died."

"Oh, sorry." Jack let his head drop for a second, then looked back up. "Then, your father's claim is yours, right? You inherited it, right?"

A hundred thoughts swirled around Will at the same time. *Inherited?* He hadn't considered that there would be *any* inheritance. Not after seeing the devastation of the homestead. Was there anything left to inherit?

Will was determined to find out.

CHAPTER

SEVEN

As the sun was teasing the mountaintops surrounding the town, Will was finishing up his last delivery of newspapers. He took the cart back to the Enterprise offices just as Jacobs was locking up the back room.

"Sam, shut it down for the night," Will heard Jacobs call out. Jacobs continued muttering. "That young man will be the death of me."

"Good evening, sir," Will said, rinsing his hands at the washbasin. "I won't be but a minute. And what time should I be here tomorrow?"

Jacobs tapped his foot impatiently, ready to close the office. He appeared indignant about having to wait on underlings. Heaving a long sigh, he cocked his head toward Will. "You're to be here before dawn. The morning edition is ready to load and deliver by six. See that you're here before that."

"In the morning?" Will asked, but then saw that Jacobs was dead serious about the time. "Yes, sir, I'll be here."

The men walked to the front door together, and Sam joined them

42

on the front steps as Jacobs closed up and shoved his keys into his pocket.

"Mr. Jacobs," Sam asked, "I was wondering if you'd given any thought to my request for a letter of recommendation to the editors in San Francisco. I truly feel that sharing my articles with their paper would help put the Territorial Enterprise on the map, globally speaking."

"Hogwash," Jacobs spat out. "You want me to recommend you to them to further your own career. You don't care two widow's mites about the Enterprise. You think too highly of yourself, Sam. Of your writing."

"Sir, I—"

"Let me tell you one thing, Sam," Jacobs' cheeks grew even redder than usual. "You'll never be more than a two-bit rag reporter, and only *that* by my good graces. You should be grateful I allow you a byline. If you really wanted to become a famous writer, you wouldn't cling to that ridiculous nom de plume." Jacobs paused for a moment as if he wanted to be sure he'd crushed poor Sam's dreams completely. "I'll see you two in the morning." And he sauntered off into the night.

Will eyed Sam sympathetically. "I wouldn't be discouraged by one man's words. Way I see it, he must think you're a good writer because he doesn't want to share you or lose you to another paper."

Sam pulled a slim cigar from his jacket pocket and tapped Will on the shoulder with it. "You, my good man, have a firm grasp of reality and a sure air of discernment that will serve you well in this cosmos. May I buy you a drink at the Palace?

"I'd be honored," Will said. "But I must tell you, I can't repay the favor until Jacobs pays me."

"Then it's a good thing that a reporter's currency is favors. I'm sure we'll be fast friends, Mr.?"

"Bancroft. I'm Will Bancroft. Good to meet you, Sam."

They ambled across the street to the saloon. Unlike at the noon hour, the grand room was already filled with men smoking, drinking, and gambling. The tables had no empty chairs, and even the bar space was limited.

Sam pointed to a gap at one end. "Let us repose to this welcoming niche."

Will followed, unsure of what Sam had actually said. A man was hammering at a piano on the other side of the room, and Will thought perhaps some distance from him might help him hear a little better.

Sam slid up to the bar and turned his body to get a full view of the room, with Will facing him. To Sam's back, Will could see another man, hunched over a frothy mug. When the red-bearded barman noticed the men, he hurried to serve them.

Sam leaned toward him and directed with his cigar. "We'll each have a shot of your best bourbon."

Redbeard nodded and poured out the bronzed liquid into the glasses. He set the bottle just beyond their reach.

"Salut," Sam said, hoisting his glass into the air.

Will matched his stance, and so did the man behind Sam. The three of them tipped their drinks back in one fluid movement.

Sam turned to the hunched man. "My name is Sam, and this gentleman is Will. And by what moniker do you make yourself known?"

The man carefully placed his glass back down on the polished wood bar top. "Ah! Bonsoir, messieurs. My name is Alois."

Will and Sam both tried to mimic his pronunciation but failed miserably. "You're a Frenchman, correct?"

"Oui, I am." His wiry blond hair came almost to his shoulders, and his clothing looked too big for his frame.

Sam tapped on his shoulder with a nod and a broad smile. "We'll call you Frenchie. You see, in America, when you are bestowed with a nickname, it is like a welcoming ceremony into a brotherhood."

Frenchie nodded. "Oui, la fraternité!"

Will offered his hand. "I'm new to Virginia City—well, back here after a few years away." He shook Frenchie's hand heartily. "How long have you been here?"

"I've been in the city for a few months. I came looking for someone, and I have found her."

"A woman?" Will asked. "In a way, I came back for a woman, too."

Sam stepped back from the bar to observe both men at the same time. He gestured to Frenchie. "You say you found your woman." He turned and regarded Will. "What about you? Did you find your woman, Will?"

Will dropped his chin and slumped his shoulders. "No. I found that my woman had left Virginia City for back East." Will held his palm up to Sam. "And what of you? Do you have a woman here?"

Straightening his back and raising his thick brow, Sam tapped his cigar on his bottom lip, skimming the edge of his mustache. "The story is my mistress. Tempting me into dark shadows and luring me into the unknown."

Tossing his head back, Will laughed. "You don't have a girl, either."

"Not yet, no."

Frenchie laughed, too. "Well, the woman I found is not mine to have."

"Star-crossed?" Sam asked. "Bad luck."

Listening to the other men, Will took a quick sweep of the room. It seemed to be filling with men by the minute.

"Bad luck, maybe, but not for me," Frenchie said in a lower tone.

More men poured through the front door, and Will wondered if this was normal for the Palace. "Is there something going on? I've never seen a saloon so filled."

Sam and Frenchie exchanged a quick glance.

"You shall see, my friend." Sam poked the cigar into his mouth and finally lit the end.

Redbeard scurried back to their end of the bar and refilled their glasses. "Ten minutes," he muttered as he rushed away to tend to others.

"Ten minutes for what?" Will asked.

Sam only smiled and puffed on his smoke.

Raising his glass again, Will mimicked the toast with a "Salut" and gulped another shot. As he placed the glass on the bar, he saw a petite blonde woman squatted down, looking for something beneath the bar. His heart lunged in his chest. She looked like Kate.

But when she stood, he saw that she was dressed like a dancer, her skirts hitched up on one side, and the ruffles cut low over her bosom. Her lips were stained blood red, and her cheeks carried an unnatural blush. It wasn't Kate.

Trying to focus on something else, Will turned his attention to the poker game at the table nearest the bar. He could see the hands of the two men facing away from him. *Decent hands*, he thought. He raised his gaze to the man on the other side of the table, who happened to be staring directly at him. The man shook his head and folded.

"Cheat!" hollered one of the men with a good hand of cards.

Will tried to turn back to the bar before anyone noticed him, but it was too late. The man jumped to his feet and whirled Will around by his shoulder.

"I'm sorry. I didn't mean to cause trouble. I was just admiring your hand. I didn't know he was watching me." Will rushed his explanation, hoping not to get hit.

Sheriff Gregory stepped between Will and the angry man. "Slow down, Evert. He's just a kid. He didn't mean no harm. And you should know better than to hold your cards out where the whole world can see 'em. Let's go easy on him, and I'll buy you a drink."

Evert seemed to think that was a fair trade, and after sneering at Will, he returned to his chair.

The commotion drew more attention to Will than he liked, so he turned back to face the bottles lined up across the back of the bar. From the corner of his eye, he saw the blonde woman staring at him.

Though the gaudy makeup and lewd dress were all wrong, the pale green eyes were exactly right.

"Kate," he called out without thinking.

The woman immediately looked down and hurried away to the dining room beyond the stairs. Will started to follow her, but Gregory stopped him in place. "Tonight, son, you're going to see the seventh wonder of the world."

"Eighth," Sam corrected. "There were already seven wonders. This would be the eighth."

The piano player began a new tune, and the room seemed to hush with anticipation. Will looked at Frenchie, who had a ravenous look in his eyes. He turned to Sam, who squinted as if he was studying for a test.

"You can look, Bancroft, but you cannot touch. Not a finger. Not a breath. Understand, kid?" Gregory's voice was firm.

Will did not understand anything. Not until Gregory stepped aside, allowing Will to view the woman at the top of the stairway.

The woman descended the steps as if she was floating on a cloud, wearing only stockings tied just above her knees and a black ribbon around her neck. The rest of her alabaster skin was bared to the world. At her appearance, every man stood at attention.

Her black hair was twisted into curls that cascaded over one shoulder, and her glistening ruby lips were pursed as if ready for a kiss. Her black eyes flashed from one man to another, around the room.

"Heard tell Madame Juliette Boulay earns one thousand dollars a night," Sam whispered only loud enough for Will to hear. "She comes down like this every month or so to pick someone new. It's like a lottery."

Will couldn't help but stare at her. Her white, perfect skin glowed. Her arms and legs were long and graceful. Every man appeared to be mesmerized by her perfect breasts and seductive loin.

"Perfection," Will could hear in whispers rising around the room.

"Devil," he heard Frenchie murmur.

The naked woman reached the floor and began a serpentine dance between the tables of men, who seemed to take extra precautions not to touch her.

Will felt a guilty flush rise from the soles of his feet, sending his nethers into motion. The madame was moving in his direction, and he crossed his hands in front of himself to hide his arousal.

"See, kid, I could tell you were lucky," Gregory whispered, nudging Will in his ribs.

Juliette's gaze settled on Will, looking him over from head to toe. She smiled wickedly and reached out, placing her sinewy fingers on his cheek.

An audible gasp rose from every other man in the room. "I've never seen her touch someone before," Sam said.

Will's knees began to shake. His heart pounded so loudly in his chest, he could hear nothing else. Juliette reached for his hand and placed it between her breasts, over her heart. "I choose you," she said with a graveled voice.

Daring to look into Juliette's eyes, Will felt his nerves overtaking him. A movement just over Juliette's shoulder caught his attention. The blonde woman was staring at him with tears in her eyes.

Kate.

Will snatched his hand away from Juliette, and without a word, he ran from the saloon into the blackness of the night.

CHAPTER

EIGHT

Narrator's Aside Note:

At this point, most readers might find this turn of events quite difficult to believe. I can tell you, as an eyewitness to the incident, I was more than a tad befuddled myself. It would have been an understatement to suggest that every other man in the establishment would have given his right hand, perhaps something even dearer, to have been chosen by Madame Boulay.

When young William forfeited that opportunity, especially in that manner, he became, in an instant, the most notorious man in Virginia City. His name was on every man's tongue, and the gossip within the saloon was something akin to a widows' quilting bee, with every lascivious accusation the imagination might ponder. By the next morning, word had spread like poison ivy throughout the whole town.

Jacobs had even asked me to write a story about the occurrence, but I assured him that the details were not suitable for a respectable tabloid such as the Territorial Enterprise. Though that was true, it was on that very night that I began taking copious notes for this exposé.

While an article on this affair might have sold a few extra papers, it was the successive events that created the bigger uprising. For before the other men had a moment to question the young man's presence of mind at denying himself the carnal pleasures offered by the madame, the woman in question raised an infernal curse against him for such a public humiliation.

As Bancroft was still in flight, Madame Boulay began a demonic incantation punctuated with furious steps of retreat up the grand staircase. Every man still watched and waited for what might happen next; these were unprecedented times.

She took no man with her, though Sheriff Gregory followed her up. He kept his tone low and unintelligible, but to my refined ears, it took on the distinct air of groveling.

Troublesome times were upon us, indeed.

CHAPTER
NINE

Will ran until he felt his knees shaking and fearing he might lose consciousness and be overtaken by a devil, he stopped and found a shadow to hide within. His heart slammed against his ribs, and he could hear nothing but his lungs wheezing labored breaths in and out. His whole body was soaked with perspiration. His mind raced.

He rested for several minutes, squatting with his back pressed against the rough brick veneer of an apparently empty building, ready to launch back into a sprint if necessary. He saw nobody on the street. He had escaped for now.

Staring at the palm of his hand—the hand that had touched the madame's body—he felt sick at his stomach. At the moment he touched her, he had expected to feel warmth. At least as warm as his own body. But he didn't. She felt cool to touch. Not like ice, but as someone who has stayed out in the brisk wind for too long.

But it might have been his imagination. He tried to think back to the exact moment. Had he seen Kate before Juliette took his hand, or after? Was it a side-effect of guilt and shame? That was undoubtedly what he felt when he saw Kate's tears.

His stomach lurched again, and he turned his head quickly to vomit whiskey-flavored bile into the grass.

Will took several deep breaths and waited for another purge, praying for mercy on his hands and knees. Nothing else came up after several dry heaves, and he decided to see if he could stand.

Rocking his body back, he steadied himself on his heels before pushing his frame upright. More deep breaths. He pressed his fingers against the bricks, feeling the heat from the afternoon sun fading slowly into the night. His fingertips throbbed. He had to walk. To get away from the stench of the whiskey. Will needed to walk and think.

Unsure of where he was going, he found himself looking up into the painted sign marked *Virginia City Livery*. Will hurried to the closed door to see if anyone was inside. High on the door was a short but wide slit with bars every few inches, creating a way to peek into the dark stable. Will peered in, clicking his tongue in the side of his cheek to get Tiger's attention.

His eyes slowly adjusted from the moonlight in the street to the darkness of the livery. He saw no people, only a hint of movement from one of the stalls. He clicked again. Soon the outline of two horses came into view. The one nearer him was a dark bay. The horse was much bigger than Tiger. As soon as the horse saw Will, it snorted and pulled his head back into his stall.

The second horse was black with a glowing white blaze running from between his ears to his nose. Unlike the first horse, he seemed interested in Will's attention. The horse pushed himself against the stall door, causing it to whine and squeak.

"Whoa, boy. Settle down." Will scanned for Tiger but saw nothing but dark.

Blaze kept pushing and scraping at his door and suddenly began a high-pitched neigh. Will shushed him several times, but the horse didn't stop. It was too much noise, and Will was sure that someone was going to hear the commotion. He'd be picked up, probably for trying to break into the stables, and he'd be right back in jail. No, he had to go.

As he walked down the quiet road, Will felt a well of frustration and anger churning inside him. Tiger was gone. His parents were gone. His home—everything was gone.

He walked. With tears burning behind his eyes and hate burning in his gut, he walked. Past businesses, past houses, past wagons, and barns, he walked. With his fingernails digging into the palms of his hands, he walked.

When his eyes finally cleared and his fists finally relaxed, Will looked around to see where he was. He found himself on the far corner of his father's homestead, looking out over the valley toward the Shoshone settlement. He saw the shacks and tents aglow from within and a small campfire burning at one side. Joseph.

William took a long, steady breath and began his descent into the ravine. This was his childhood playground. This was the Virginia City he knew. As he approached the notch in the ridge, he slowed his pace. He was on high alert.

The moon was almost perfectly full and as white as a dove. He felt something move nearby—saw a rustling in the sage, heard a twig snap a few yards in front of him.

He became acutely aware that he had nothing with which he could defend himself. Not a gun nor a knife. He hunched down, feeling his knees tremble.

Had he been followed? Was this a wolf? Something else?

Another snap, but this time from behind.

Will spun around, coming within inches of a hulking silhouette with glowing white teeth.

"What are you doing out here by yourself?" a graveled voice asked.

A yelp escaped Will's throat as he recognized the man as Joseph's uncle, Ten Skies. "Blast!" Will gasped. "You scared me."

The man had almost no reaction. "Joseph said you were back."

"I saw a campfire. I thought maybe he was out here." Will held out his arm to Ten Skies. "It's good to see you again."

Ten Skies looked at Will's hand but didn't take it. "Come with me." He led Will down the slope until they were just a few yards from the fire outside of camp. "Take off your clothes."

Balking at the suggestion, Will looked around for his friend. "Where is Joseph? I just wanted to talk to him for a moment."

"No," the older man said.

"Please?" Will wasn't sure what kind of manners he was supposed to use with a Shoshone medicine man these days.

"Take off your clothes." Ten Skies stared at Will impatiently.

Crossing his arms over his chest, Will scowled and searched the darkness. "Why do I have to take off my clothes?"

"Because you're carrying a curse in them." Joseph stepped out of the darkness and into the firelight. "My uncle will cleanse you, but first, you have to give him your clothes."

Will started to laugh and then saw Ten Skies and Joseph exchange a tired glance. "Are you serious?"

Joseph nodded. "Before we could see you coming, we could see the curse. It stands over you like a ghost. Ten Skies has everything ready. Just give him your clothes and follow us to the creek."

"My shirt, then?" Will asked.

"Everything. Anything the sheriff gave you." Joseph shook his head. "Look, I don't like it any better than you. But it's got to be done."

Will began the undressing, and Ten Skies directed him to pile the cursed clothing into a wide flat basket on the ground. Once Will was completely naked, Ten Skies seemed satisfied.

"Follow," he said. He picked up the basket and walked the ten paces to a creek where a crescent of rocks formed a pool of relatively calm water. The man pointed to the pool. "Get in."

A laugh sprang from his lips before he could stop it. "I'm naked, and it's cold. I don't want to stand in icy water. I could get sick and die."

Joseph shook his head. "You think this is all a joke. We have better things to do than watch a scrawny white man dance naked in the river. You may die, but it won't be from sickness. You touched a devil tonight. You have a curse ten feet tall riding on your shoulders. Do you want our help or not?"

Will stared at his friend. "I have to dance naked in the river?"

Ten Skies sighed and started to walk away.

"No, wait," Will said. "What do I have to do?"

Joseph motioned back to the water. "You have to get into the pool. Be careful because it's deeper than it looks." He patted a large flat stone at the river's edge. "You can sit here and slide in."

"How deep is it?" Will asked.

"Your head will be above water." Joseph stood close, in case Will slipped, and once Will was neck-deep in the pool, he knelt beside his uncle.

Ten Skies began to chant over the clothes as Joseph took each piece from the basket and plunged it into the pool beside Will.

Will's teeth chattered, and numbness spread from the soles of his feet to his chin. The creek water splashed up into his ears, making it more difficult to hear the chanting. When all the clothes, including Will's boots, were immersed several times, Joseph brought them back out of the water and placed them into the basket again.

"Now, take a deep breath and let it out," Joseph instructed. "Do it several times until you're ready."

Will inhaled and exhaled three times before asking, "Ready for what?"

Without explanation, Joseph pushed down on Will's shoulders and held his head under the water until a colossal bubble of air broke on the surface. After that, he pulled Will out of the pool in one swift motion.

Coughing and gasping for breath, Will screeched. "You tried to kill me. You almost drowned me."

Ten Skies shook his head, carrying the basket back to the fireside. "There is no curse in your body now. You are cleansed."

At the fire, Joseph picked up a blanket and handed it to Will. "Cover up and keep warm while we finish cleansing your clothes."

Will wrapped the woolen blanket around his shoulders and

found a broad flat rock next to the flames on which to sit. "I might-a rather had the curse," he muttered between still-chattering teeth.

Ten Skies rolled his eyes. "He doesn't see what is right before him."

Joseph held up his hands to his uncle. "All the more reason he needs our help."

Taking a cigar-sized bundle of wrapped leaves from his leather pouch, Ten Skies held them at the edge of the fire until they began to smoke with a pale blue plume. He waved the plume over the boots first, chanting again. Next, the socks and the underwear, then the bandana and the string tie. Lastly, he chanted over the pants and shirt.

"Stand up and open the blanket," Ten Skies directed. "No laughter."

Will didn't dare smile. He got to his feet and let his arms drop to his sides, leaving the blanket dangling loosely from his fingers. The medicine man chanted and waved the smoke just inches from Will's skin, starting at his feet and working around his body, lingering at his heart and his head.

"You are cleansed now. Don't let yourself get cursed again." And with that, Ten Skies walked back to his home, leaving Joseph and Will at the fire.

"Thank you," Will called out, but Joseph shook his head.

"Let's get your clothes dry. You can't go back to town naked." Joseph laughed.

Will held his underwear over the fire until it was only slightly damp and then pulled it on while working on his pants. Joseph had put two long river-soaked sticks into the fire and settled Will's boots upside-down over them to speed up their drying.

"How did your uncle know I had touched the madame? I'm guessing that's who he calls the devil."

Joseph nodded. "He could see it on your hand when you held it out to shake his. He recognizes it easily now. Not as rare as it used to be."

"Did she put the curse on me?" Will squeezed out the last drops of water from his socks, and they sizzled on the embers.

Joseph nodded. "She's not what you think she is. If you touched her without her permission—"

Will shook his head excitedly. "No, it wasn't like that. She came down the stairs, bare as the day she was born, and she came to me. She took my hand. She put it on her body."

His mouth agape, Joseph released a short cough. "What? She chose you?"

Nodding, Will whispered. "But I didn't. I mean, I didn't go with her. I ran."

Plopping down on the flat rock, Joseph looked up at Will with wild eyes. "You ran?"

"Yes, I'm telling you. I ran away. I hid. I threw up. I tried to find Tiger, but he was gone. I just kept going until I was here." Will sunk down to sit beside his friend. "And maybe the worst part of it all, I saw Kate. I think I saw her. I'm not sure."

"Did she see you?" Joseph asked.

"Yes. She looked right at me." Will's voice cracked. "That's why I ran."

Joseph tossed Will's shirt to his side and let his face drop into his hands. "You not only touched Madame Boulay, but you also insulted her in front of the city. And you saw Kate."

"I'm pretty sure it was her."

"It was her." Joseph sighed. He looked Will directly in the eyes. "What's left of her."

TEN

"I have to go back there," Will explained. He was clothed again, except for his boots. "For Kate and for Tiger."

Joseph shook his head. "Kate is lost, brother. She sold herself to Madame. If you go back for her, you will get the both of you killed."

Will scowled into the flames. "She's not lost. You didn't see her. She had tears in her eyes."

"Because she knows what will happen to you. She's a day-walker. That means she's not entirely gone. She does Madame's bidding day and night, but her will is not her own." Joseph stoked the fire with a stick. "I know you like her, Will, but she's lost to you."

"She still has my heart." Will watched the sparks rise up to the stars.

"Maybe, but someone else has her soul." Joseph sighed. "I say you should leave Virginia City. I could go with you."

"You can't leave your uncle. He's training you to be the next Medicine Man."

"Yeah, that's working out well for me. Every time I go to town, I get arrested. When I stay with our tribe, I'm called the traitor. My own people think I'm trying to sell them out to the white man. They won't see that there are benefits to be had through cooperation—things to be learned from both communities."

"You must be the one to bring them together." Ten Skies' voice echoed in the darkness, startling both young men.

"Uncle, we thought you left."

Ten Skies ignored the remark. "There must be some sort of harmony if both cultures are to thrive. Only someone like you—who sees the good in both—will achieve that kind of union."

Will nodded. "You see, you can't leave, either."

"But you can, and you should." Joseph sighed. "Uncle, tell him."

Ten Skies looked up and to the east, where a purple haze was pushing into the black. "Unfortunately, William is right. He must go back."

"He'll be killed," Joseph argued.

"I won't be killed," Will said resolutely.

"He may die," Ten Skies said, causing Will's brows to rise. "But he must be the one to fight her. He has his eyes open now. He humiliated her. She will be blinded with a burning rage. She will make mistakes."

Will stood and faced Ten Skies, vehemently shaking his head. "I am not going to fight the madame. She is a woman. And I didn't mean to humiliate her. I just couldn't do what she was trying to get me to do." He raked his hands through his dark hair. "And what do you mean that I may die?"

Sitting down in the dirt by the fading fire, Ten Skies spoke without looking at either of the other men. "I called her a devil. But she is perhaps more of a witch. She drinks the blood of humans to keep herself young forever. With their blood in her veins, she can control them. She has the power to decide what they do and how long they should live."

"She drinks blood?" Will asked. His stomach dropped.

Ten Skies barely paused. "If Madame devours a person—drinks

all of their blood—they will die. If she drinks a little at a time, she controls them."

"They become a day-walker," Joseph interjected.

Will plopped back down on the rock beside Ten Skies and stared at the older man. It was like listening to a fantastic ghost story as a child, but Will knew that the man believed every word he was saying.

"And if Madame shares her blood with a victim, they become one. Both will live forever." Ten Skies shook his head. "But it is not a life worth living. Madame is never satisfied. She will always crave more. More blood, more life, more pleasure, and no matter what she does, it will never be enough."

Joseph scoffed. "And why should we stay? At some point, she'll consume the whole city."

"That is why you must stay. That is why we all must fight." Ten Skies took his turtle shell pouch from his belt and opened it in the glow of the fire. "Will, you must face her and fight her. You have lost the most to her. You have the most to gain from her defeat."

Turning his back to Will, Joseph muttered. "You only suspect, Uncle. You don't know."

"Don't know what?" Will asked.

"What Madame has already taken from you," Ten Skies answered.

Joseph whirled around to interrupt. "Uncle! You say that Madame will make mistakes because of the rage against Will. If you tell him, you will put that same rage into his heart. He will make mistakes. And he is young. She has decades, maybe centuries more experience over him. Why do you think he'll be able to control his rage better than Madame?"

"Because I will equip him. He will be able to see her for what she is."

Will struggled for a break to ask his question. When the pause came, he jumped in. "What is it you have to tell me?"

Ten Skies looked up at the fading stars for a second and then back to Will. "You should know that Madame Boulay killed your parents."

Will felt like he was back under the water in the river pool, gasping for air.

Joseph shook his head. "Ten Skies doesn't know that. He suspects it, but that's all."

"The same way I knew that you had touched Madame." Ten Skies' tone remained even as he settled his gaze back on the flames. Without looking down, he fingered the beads and flasks from his pouch. "The same way I know that you must be the one to face her."

Releasing a series of several short breaths, Will grabbed the sides of his head with his hands and pulled at his hair. Juliette Boulay murdered his parents? She did this only hours before he came back home? Will's thoughts were scattered and confused. His first impulse was to run again, but Kate was still in Madame's power. And Tiger was hidden somewhere in the city. He would have to stay. He had to fight. Another question popped into Will's mind and out of his mouth. "And is this the same way you know that I may die?"

The medicine man pressed his lips into a thin, straight line. "Life and death are not as easy to see in this case. Is Madame alive? Is she dead? The question can be asked about all of her day-walkers. And the same with her blood-sisters. But good and evil are easy to see." Ten Skies raised a flask of golden liquid into the light. The amber-filled bottle almost glowed in the pre-dawn chill. "I will give you my vision. I will provide you with protection against the vile demons of air and fire. You will have everything you need to defeat her. The rest is up to you."

CHAPTER

ELEVEN

With the sky just beginning to lighten into a violet arc in the east, Will ambled down the main street before the town woke. The roads were almost empty, and shopkeepers swept the front stoops, eyeing him suspiciously. He tried to raise a hand in greeting when he made eye contact, but most simply looked away or went inside.

He had decided it was best to go about his business as if he knew nothing about a curse, or Madame Boulay's treachery, or anything else for that matter. The longer he walked, the more confident he became that his ignorance was a fact. If he hadn't met up with Joseph and Ten Skies last night, he'd have never been told their suspicions. And indeed, that's all it was.

Juliette Boulay was just a woman, after all. Not a monster or devil. Not a witch or a phantom. He had seen her. He'd seen all of her. He had actually touched her.

A shiver shot down his spine at the thought.

"Best not think about it," he muttered to himself.

Another twenty yards and he stood frozen in the middle of the street. On one side of him was the Palace. On the other, the Enter-

62

prise. He swallowed hard and looked up to the window of the bedroom that was to be his. Dark.

A noise spun him around to face the Enterprise. His friend Sam stood at the door. "You're still alive?"

Will heaved a louder-than-expected sigh of relief. "Yeah, for now. Though another scare like that might just do me in."

"Well, come on. Jacobs will be here soon." Sam opened the door and glanced at his pocket watch as Will hurried past.

Wanting information, yet dreading what he might hear, Will dared to ask. "What happened after I ran out?"

Sam's lip curled on one side, giving his mustache a crooked slant. "Nothing much," Sam said as the men walked through to the newsroom.

Will sighed again. "That's good to hear."

A chuckle burst through Sam's lips. "It would be if it were true. Unfortunately, I am a master at concocting half-truths and fantastical falsehoods. And delivering said lies without a hint of deceptive intent."

"Ugh," Will's tone deflated. "Then what did happen?"

"Before or after Madame Boulay raced upstairs?"

"Before?" Will looked around as he saw Jack and another boy enter.

Sam waited for the young men to go back. "She said some extremely unflattering things about your manhood, your parentage, and your upbringing."

Will's face flushed red with a cocktail of embarrassment and anger. "And after?"

"Afterward? Let's say the madame flew up the stairs in quite a fluster, followed closely by your friend, Sheriff Gregory. The other saloon guests stayed silent for a minute or two, waiting to see if anything else might happen." Sam paused when the front door opened and closed with a bang. "Get to the back now, and we can talk later."

Hurrying through the door to the back room, Will found the boys in a huddle around the door, trying to hear over the sound of the printer. They scattered as he entered.

As Will walked to the back wall to link the carts together, he felt the eyes of everyone in the room on his back. How could they possibly know anything about last night? It happened just a few hours ago. And they were children.

When he turned around to face them, each one looked down and began to work on their first bundles.

The door between the offices opened again, and Will heard Jacobs yell at Sam. The round man stuck his head through the door. "Bancroft, my office!"

Some of the younger boys started to laugh. Jack stopped them with a quick admonition. "Keep your hands busy, lads, or you could be called in next."

Will nodded a quick thanks to Jack and paced through to Jacob's office.

"Yes, sir?" Will stood just inside the man's door, sure he was about to be fired.

Jacobs straightened up in his chair and stared into the young man's eyes. "I heard what happened last night, son."

Licking his dry lips, Will tried to assemble a defense. "Sir, I—"

"Now, let me finish. And have a seat." He gestured to the wooden chair opposite his at the desk. "You're new to town, so I will give you the benefit of the doubt. But you need to understand a few things." He pulled at his collar, and a glisten of sweat showed on his forehead. "Madame does not appreciate being..." He stammered as if he couldn't remember the right words. "We don't tell Madame no."

Dropping his head to his chest, Will whispered, "I understand now. It won't happen again."

Jacobs fumbled with a pencil on his blotter. "I should hope so. Or rather, I should hope not. It's not good for the paper. Bad for our reputation. Bad for circulation."

Watching the man stumble over himself, Will noticed something strange. Inside the cuff of Jacobs' left sleeve was another cuff. Like a loose bandage, but it was black. Will couldn't see if it was attached to another sleeve or only a strap of some kind. He gestured and started to ask Jacobs if he'd been in an accident, but before he could form the question, Jacobs noticed his interest and dropped his left hand into his lap behind the desk.

"Son, I want you to take this as a warning. We here in Virginia City have a lot of respect for Madame Boulay. She has helped us in ways you may not understand."

Will hurried a statement into the conversation. "I'd like to, though. Understand, I mean."

Jacobs's face lightened a bit.

"If you please, sir, I'd really like to hear about the ways she's helped." Will leaned forward with an eager expression on his face. He hoped the older man would keep talking.

It seemed to work. "Well, of course," Jacobs said. He looked pleased to be the one recounting the town's history with the madame. "A year or so ago, the Shoshone attacked. The savages took a couple of the young girls and a few horses, too. Madame joined the posse to go after them. All by herself, she shot one of the Indians and got the girls back. The horses were lost, but the rest of the posse was able to bring most of the raiders to justice. Four Shoshone were hanged, and Madame was officially deputized."

Will nodded. Of course, she was, he thought. Jacobs continued, now on a roll.

"And then there was the fire earlier this week. It was upon us before we knew it, and Madame was right out there with the men, passing buckets and keeping the town safe. You may not have heard yet, but Madame is being lauded at a ceremony tomorrow for her bravery. She'll be made the honorary Fire Chief for helping fight the fire at the Bancroft land." Jacobs stopped for a moment and looked at Will. "Bancroft? Were they kin?"

"They were my parents, sir." Will's voice still cracked every time he said the words.

Jacobs fixed an expression of contrition on his face. "I'm sorry, son. I didn't know." He looked down at his lap for a second. "Well, then, I suppose you owe a great debt of gratitude to her, too. Let's just see that your accidental disrespect doesn't repeat itself."

"Yes, sir," Will said automatically. The fire in his gut spread up through his chest and down his arms. He needed to stay in control. He needed to keep his job to remain part of the town. He needed to keep an eye on Boulay. He needed to find Tiger. He needed to talk to Kate. None of that would happen if he went off half-cocked.

He pushed the fury down.

"Now, get back to work, son." Jacobs shooed him out of his office with a flick of his wrist.

Will nodded and returned to the printing room, passing Sam's desk on the way.

"Glad you won't be leaving us yet," Sam said as Will tapped on the corner of the desk.

"Not quite yet."

The boys were working on their bundles, pushing the twined ones to the edge of the table, ready for Will to load onto the carts. He started at the near end and worked his way down the line, finishing the first round in front of Jack.

"I thought you were a goner for sure," Jack said. "You must have some mystical power to still be here."

Will shook his head, though the idea no longer sounded ridiculous to him. "He just gave me a warning. And I'll be more careful next time."

One of the other boys muttered, "I heard she don't give any man a chance for a next time."

Jack rolled his eyes. "You're a dope, Gray. Since Will is the first man to ever tell Madame no, I guess she's never had to offer anyone a second chance."

"You all are too young to be talking about this, anyway. Get back to work, or Jacobs will turn us all out on the streets." Will started back down the table for the second load.

Gray wrinkled his nose. "I'm not too young for anything. I'll be thirteen next month. And I can talk and work at the same time. Anyone who says I can't will get a taste of my fist."

Jack shrugged and tied up his next bundle. The other boys worked in silence, which gave Gray nothing to say, making him more upset.

Will loaded all the carts quickly and had the other bundles stacked and waiting at the back door. He waited for the last few stacks to be picked up, and Jack joined him.

"Do you think she'll be mad?" he asked Will.

"You're talking about Boulay?" Will shrugged. "She probably will, but I can't do anything about that now, can I?"

Jack sighed. He stood with his back straight, and Will thought the boy might even be stretching a bit to stand eye to eye with him. Jack's mouth twitched before he spoke. "I guess you could talk to her. Maybe apologize. Maybe pay her fee and... make friends with her."

Will grinned, trying to remember if he was ever so young and naïve. "Listen, I appreciate the fact that you're worried for me. I really do. But even if I had a thousand dollars just sitting around, she's not the type of woman I'm looking for." Will swallowed hard, trying not to think too much about Boulay. "But thanks for being such a good friend to me."

Jack scowled. "You should think about what I said. She has a lot of influence in Virginia City. You don't want to be on her bad side."

Blinking back his surprise at Jack's response, Will nodded. "So I've heard."

"Have you young men finished for the morning?" Jacobs called from behind them. "I have a letter that I need to have delivered to Fitz at the bank.

Jack shoved his hands into his pockets. "My mother is delivering my lunch soon. She said I needed to be here."

Will raised his hand. "I'd be happy to take it for you, sir, just as soon as the rest of the papers are picked up. I'll go right by the bank on my deliveries."

Jacobs nodded. "Jack, why don't you wait for the bundles to be loaded." Jacobs held up an envelope. "Bancroft, here is my message. Do you know Mr. Fitz?"

Thinking back to his younger days, Will thought about the middle-aged man with the bald head and pronounced limp. "Is he the one with no..." Manners dictated that he didn't mention his premature balding. "Uhm, the gentleman with the..." Or the limp. But Will had already shifted his weight to one side and cocked his head to match.

"That's him," Jacobs said, handing Will an envelope sealed with dark blue wax. "He'll be in the right-side office in the front of the bank. "And, son, it's a very important message. Please don't lose it along the way."

"Yes, sir," Will said, taking the message. He was beginning to dislike being called son by all the men in town. He'd never hear his own father call him that again, and it was starting to wear on his nerves when others did.

Taking the letter, Will waved good-bye to Jack and pulled the laden cart behind him. He stopped at each station along the way, leaving an extra bundle for each boy, as needed. He finally dropped his last load of papers at the corner in front of the bank entrance.

As he ascended the steps to the bank entrance, he removed his hat and raked his fingers through his hair. He retrieved the letter from his breast pocket and took a deep breath as he went inside. Straight ahead, he saw the tellers on duty, both visiting with customers. To his left, an older man sat at a desk reading through a stack of papers. To his right, he saw a closed door marked PRIVATE. He straightened his spine and tapped.

"Yes?" came a slow tenor voice.

"I have a message for you from Mr. Jacobs at the Enterprise."

"Come in. Come in," the voice chirped.

Will entered, holding out the letter in his left hand. Mr. Fitz stood and passed a white handkerchief over his bald head. Will reached out his right hand to shake Fitz's. "It's good to see you again, Mr.

Fitz. I've been a long time away from Virginia City, but it's good to see a familiar face."

Fitz shook Will's hand with slight hesitation. He squinted and leaned forward. "You do look familiar, son."

There it was again. He couldn't let it bother him. "I'm William Bancroft, sir. Victor's son."

Fitz nodded and then smiled. "That's right. Why I'd know you anywhere. You're the spitting image of Victor." His expression quickly dissolved into a frown. "I'm sorry to hear about your parents. Yes, you have been away for a long while. Are you here to pay your respects?"

Will handed the envelope to Fitz and bowed his head. "Something like that." Will acted as though he had just been struck with an idea. "I don't suppose my father had any money deposited with your bank or anything else here for safe-keeping?"

Twitching his narrow lips from one side to another, Fitz grimaced. "As a matter of fact, I believe he did have something with us. I would usually ask for a letter of kinship, but under the circumstances, I suppose we can dismiss that." He scribbled something on a notepad. "Take this to either one of the tellers, and they'll take care of you."

As Will took the slip of paper from his hand, he noticed a black cuff up the man's sleeve. "Thank you, sir." Will paused before leaving. "Do you need me to take back a reply to Mr. Jacobs?"

Fitz glanced down at the letter in his hand and back to Will. "No, son. That won't be necessary. Thank you."

Offering a slight bow on his way out, Will closed the door, holding tight to the note in his hand. He stepped up to the window closest to him, and the woman nodded without speaking.

"Good day," Will said, handing her the note. He guessed that the woman was a few years older than him. Her expression was dull as if she was resigned to a job she resented while she waited for something exciting to happen.

She read the note and looked back at Will nervously. "One

moment, sir." She passed the note to the other teller. The man read it, blinked, and then stepped over to the woman's window.

"I'm sorry, sir, but this account is empty."

Will gestured to Mr. Fitz's office. "But he just told me—"

"I understand," the man said, interrupting. "But Sheriff Gregory was just here—while you were in with Mr. Fitz—and emptied the account. He said it was a matter of law."

"Thank you." Will's words fell out against his will. He stepped out of the bank and back into the sunlight. How could Gregory do that? How could he know? Will marched back to his empty cart and started toward the Enterprise. "He can't get away with that."

He pulled his hat low over his eyes and stopped when he realized who was standing right in front of him. Gregory.

"Get away with what, son?"

CHAPTER

TWELVE

"Sheriff Gregory, just the man I wished to speak to." Will's voice held steady against the nerves he felt inside.

"I'm here to help with whatever you may need." Gregory's tone was relaxed and as confident as ever. "Would you like to come back to my office?"

Gesturing to the hand cart, Will shook his head. "No, sir, I can't at the moment. I need to get back to work. By the way, I'm real grateful for the job. I like the work. Makes me feel part of the community." Will thought it was best to stay on the man's good side for as long as he could.

"I thought you might like it." Gregory rolled his cigar in his mouth with his tongue. "But you looked a bit upset just now. Why don't you tell me what's got you riled up, and I'll see if I can fix it." He motioned toward the Enterprise. "I'll walk you back."

As they ambled back to the newspaper office, Will breathed deep to catch whatever stray courage may be floating in the air. "I was just in the bank to see about my father's account."

Before he could say another word, Gregory interrupted. "While you were on the clock, you were conducting personal business?"

Will shook his head. "Not exactly. Jacobs sent me to see Mr. Fritz, and I asked him a question, and he sent me to a teller."

"I see," Gregory said.

"But when I got to the teller, I was told that you had just emptied my father's account."

The men took several more steps before the lawman answered. "Well, son, you understand why I did that, don't you?"

Will squinted as his gaze met Gregory's. "No, sir, I can't say that I do."

Gregory inhaled, expanding his chest to its extent, then huffed it back out again. "Son, it's the law. Whenever a man passes, the contents of his bank account must be held for thirty days against any debt he may owe. After that, we'll make every effort to find the next of kin to take possession of whatever is left. It's a standard legal procedure, I assure you."

"But wouldn't that be for a lawyer to do?" Will didn't know much about laws and procedures, but this seemed simple enough to him.

"Ordinarily, in a bigger city, I suppose it would. Virginia City is growing, but we don't have lawyers on every street. The few that we do have are busy. I checked with them, and none of them were associates of your father. So, rather than them taking on a whole new case that would be so temporary, I stepped in to help." Gregory made the whole situation sound like he was doing Will a favor.

Instead of arguing, Will again remained polite. "May I ask how much there was in their account?"

Gregory chomped down on the cigar. "Son, I can't disclose amounts yet. You see, I have to log it into my ledger as I count it out in front of a deputy. And then I have to inform your father's business associates that I'll be the one handling any debt payoffs. You understand?"

Will thought he might explode if Gregory called him *son* one more time. He quelled his anger and continued. "I do understand. And then after all the debts are settled, I can claim the remains of his money?"

Nodding with a fake smile spreading his mustache wide, Gregory answered. "Yes, sir. As long as you can prove that you're Victor's next of kin."

"Prove?" Will asked. How was he supposed to prove something like that?

"Yes. Legally you have to show some sort of documentation that would satisfy the law. But don't worry, Bancroft. Three sworn affidavits from people who know you will work just fine."

A brief wave of relief ran over Will. He looked up and realized he was back in front of the newspaper. "Sheriff, one last question. I went by the livery to see my horse last night, and Tiger wasn't there. Could you direct me to where he's housed, please?"

"Of course, I can. Why don't you come by my office after you're done for the day here? I have some other things to discuss with you about last night. We'll get it all ironed out, and then I'll take you to your horse." Gregory didn't wait for an answer but turned away and headed up to his post.

Waiting until Gregory was out of earshot, Will began stringing together a line of the vilest curse words he could think of. He knew his mother would have washed out his mouth with soap if she had been there, but most of the curses were a direct result of her *not* being there. "And I'm not sorry for a single one," he whispered to himself.

Looking up, he saw Sam leaning against a porch post. The reporter held up a finger in salute. "Looks like you're holding your own against the sheriff."

Will shrugged. "Hard to tell. He's always talking in circles. I can't tell if I'm getting anywhere."

Sam nodded to the back of the building and then fell in step with Will as he pulled the cart to the back door. "You're not." Sam opened the door to the back room. "But from what I can tell, neither is he."

"I'm not sure what that's supposed to mean," Will said.

Leading Will through the empty print room and into the newsroom, Sam gestured to the chair beside his desk. "What I mean, my friend, is that Gregory has ill-intentions toward you. "He is looking for the means to trip you, and as of yet, you have avoided his traps adeptly. You've kept your wits about you instead of turning on him in a rage. Which, I'm sure you are aware, is his objective."

"Why does he want me angry?"

Sam flipped open a small box on his desktop containing the slim cigars he carried. He offered Will one and took another for himself. Without lighting it, he began to roll it between his thumb and index finger. "An angry man makes mistakes."

"So I've been told," Will said, staring at the cigar in his hand.

"And when a man makes angry mistakes, his life is often upturned in turmoil. Turmoil leads to desperation. And a desperate man may take the law into his own hands. Gregory would love to see that happen to you. He would love to see you swing." Sam held his cigar under his nose for a deep breath. He then resumed his rolling. "I didn't know your father, Will, but I knew of him. He was a desperate man."

Will set his cigar on the desk and leaned forward. "Desperate, how?"

Opening the drawer in front of him, Sam withdrew a flat hand tool with three small holes across it. He put his finger and thumb into the holes on the sides and the cigar's tip through the center. A quick flex of his hand and the end snipped off and dropped to the desk blotter. Without offering the cutter to Will, Sam slipped it back into his drawer. "He was threatening the sheriff and his men. He was threatening Boulay. Nobody lasts long in Virginia City once the threats begin."

"Why was he threatening them?" Will's eyes were shifting in his head. "What were they doing to my father?"

Sam looked around the room, which was filling up again with other writers coming in for the afternoon. His tone lowered. "They wanted him to throw in his lot with them."

Will tried to match his murmur, but the excitement drove his voice a step louder. "I don't understand. My father was a miner. What could he do for the sheriff? Or for Madame Boulay?"

"Your father's mine was beginning to out-produce many of the others. He spent his silver with individuals, rather than at the General Store or saloons." Sam continued to appreciate his tobacco without actually lighting the end. "Madame Boulay has a network here in the city. Her people are careful to see that all of the silver filters through her establishment, one way or another. I've been watching and taking notes for over a year now."

"Why? Does she keep the silver?" Will asked.

"No, she's quite generous with it, once it's been in her hands." Sam finally slid the cigar into the corner of his mouth. "She likes to appear the philanthropist."

"The what?"

Sam smiled, and the cigar swung out wide. "She wants everyone to feel as though they owe her a great debt of gratitude. She loves to appear as some sort of holy mother, taking care of her children."

Will gasped. "That's downright sacrilegious."

"It's more than that, friend." Sam hunched down closer to Will and lowered his voice further. "Anyone who opposes that appearance is done away with. Utterly destroyed by her and those beneath her."

"She killed my parents?" Will asked, his voice barely audible.

"I can't say for sure." Sam shrugged. "I've been unable to discern or reveal any concrete evidence to that conclusion. But I do know that a few weeks ago, I heard a rumor that your father had agreed to sell his mine to Boulay. That assertion was vehemently denied by your father. And publicly, too."

"And now, my parents are dead."

"Sam! Bill! Get back to work!" Jacobs's voice rattled both men, and they jumped to their feet.

"Yes, sir," they said together.

They walked to the door separating their workspaces. Sam leaned closely to Will's ear. "I thought they had you last night at the saloon. Your resilience in the face of such seduction was admirable. I can't say that I would have been able to resist had I been in your place."

"I can't lie to you; I almost didn't resist." Will took a deep breath, preparing for another round of heavy lifting.

Sam nodded. "But you did. And I can't stress this enough, Will. You must watch your step. You're going to see the sheriff tonight, right?"

"Yes."

"Don't cross him. But don't succumb to his will, either."

CHAPTER

THIRTEEN

Before Will had reached the sheriff's office, he could see the smoke from Gregory's fat cigar rolling out into the street. The barrel-chested man leaned against the building, watching citizens passing from one end of town to the other. When Will approached, the lawman launched himself out to greet the young man.

"Come on inside, Bancroft. Let's get our business settled."

Will nodded. "Yes, sir. I'd like to get everything worked out, myself."

The men entered the shabby front office, and Will thought the room looked smaller than it had just two nights before. He felt less intimidated, but he reminded himself that he couldn't let his anger get the better of him.

Gregory again poured two drinks—one for each of them. He sat back in his chair with a casual air about him. "Bancroft, I have to tell you, what you did last night—running out on Madame like you did —that's put me in quite a spot. And not just with her, but the whole town."

Swallowing hard, Will shrugged, as if he'd had this conversation a thousand times already. "I don't see why my not bedding a whore makes any difference to anyone else."

Gregory yanked his cigar from between his gritted teeth and let out a hiss. "Boy, there's a whole lot that you don't see. Firstly, I had to call in some favors to get that room in the Palace for you. The room that you didn't even stay in. And whether you sleep there or not, you still owe for it. Second, you insulted Madame Boulay to her face, not to mention you calling her a whore behind her back."

"And if not a whore, then what is she?" Will let his tone rise, though his composure remained cool.

"Juliette Boulay is a prominent member of Virginia City's highest class. Tomorrow at noon, she's to be named Honorary Fire Chief for the way she helped put out the fire that took your parents. If not for her, the whole town might have been engulfed." Gregory looked as though he would come across the desk in an attack.

Will stayed reserved. "I see. So now I owe her an apology?"

"I'm not sure she'd accept it now."

"I still have no intention of bedding her." Will took a deep breath and cocked his head to one side. "And I won't be staying at the Palace, either. I'll settle my bill with you later on that account."

Gregory growled as he began again. "I don't know who you think you are, son, but—"

"I'd appreciate it if you would stop calling me son. I had a father, and you're not him." Will flexed his jaw, waiting for a slap that didn't come. He watched the sheriff's hands tremble as a fury billowed within the man. Will struggled to keep his own body calm and under control, but he remembered what Ten Skies and Sam both had warned. "Sheriff, I understand that you and others may feel beholden to Madame Boulay. But I do not."

"Maybe you don't feel beholden to her, but you most certainly are beholden to me." Gregory's nostrils flared over his black mustache. His bottom lip swelled out in a pout. "I have your father's money in my possession. I have your horse in my possession. I have your life in my hands."

Though he tried to stay calm, Will could feel a hot flush pushing up from his gut. Two nights ago, he'd been crushed and in tears. Last night, he'd been frightened and nearly drowned. But now, facing Gregory's threats, he was ready to fight. He had a choice to make. He could throw a punch and land himself back in a cell, or he could keep his composure and get his freedom back. For a split-second, he balled his fist.

But then Kate's face flashed in his mind. He thought of his mother and father, and of Tiger. Everyone he cared for had been stolen from him. And he couldn't get them back if he was dead.

"You do have my life in your hands, Sheriff. And I am grateful for the kindness you showed me. But as a man, you understand that I need some freedom, too. I'm not a child who needs to be taken care of. Maybe I was, but things are different now." Will's mind spun out a thousand ideas. "Let me handle my affairs my way. Give me a month to get you paid back. Let's just plan on settling everything when you discharge my father's estate."

Gregory's shoulders seemed to relax. As if he'd been the one to suggest it, he appeared to like the idea. "Yes, let's plan on settling everything then." He popped the cigar back into his mouth. "That will be just fine with me."

With his cigar in his right hand, Gregory picked up his drink and tilted the glass over his lips. As he did, Will caught a glimpse of a black cuff beneath his sleeve.

Will felt an uneasy knot growing in his gut. "And I'll go to collect my things from the Palace. Boulay will be happy to have the room available again."

The sheriff stood and gestured to the door. "Sure, why don't you run down there and get your belongings. But you'd better watch yourself. If Boulay sees you, she's likely to bite your head off."

Squinting at the horrific image in his head, Will rose and left the office. After he was clear of the building's shadow, he picked up his pace. He decided that if he was going to get his things—if Madame Boulay hadn't already burned them to ashes—he wanted to do that before the Palace filled with patrons. And before dark.

CHAPTER

FOURTEEN

Bancroft stood at the entry door closest to the foot of the stairs, next to the Palace dining room. He watched Redbeard hurrying with last-minute preparations for a busy night. He caught a glimpse of the blonde running down the stairs with a basket of linens. As soon as she set the load down, he stepped inside.

His presence startled her, and she clasped her hand over her mouth to stifle a scream.

Will shook his head. "I didn't mean to upset you. I'm Will Bancroft. And you're Kate Grosvenor, aren't you?"

The woman looked confused as if she didn't recognize him. She tilted her head forward and looked into his eyes.

Whatever doubt Will might have had before, it was gone now. "Kate, it's me. I've come home."

The blonde twitched her head away. "Madame took your things from the corner room and threw them into the bin. I put them into a box, just in case you came back."

"I did come back. Kate, I came back for you." Will started to reach out for her.

She leaned away from his touch. "I'll get your things, but you must go. Madame can't see you here." Without another word, Kate hurried through the dining room door and returned in just a few seconds with a tied bundle of clothes. "Now go. Right now, you must go."

Will took the wrapped clothing from her hand, letting his fingers smooth over hers. Goosebumps rose on his arm when he realized Kate's skin was chilled. "No, I can't go now. I need to talk to you. I need to see you," he said.

Kate's gaze fell away from his. "I can't. I don't know you. I'm not who you think I am."

"I *do* know you. You're my girl. My best girl, Kate." Will tucked the clothes under his arm and reached for her again. "If not now, then when may I see you?"

"Go," she answered, pulling away from his touch. She turned to run up the stairs but stopped short.

Will looked up and saw her. Madame Boulay, dressed in a crimson gown that cinched her bosom high, was descending the staircase, staring directly into his eyes.

"You have nothing for me but disdain," she said. Her voice was low and sounded like a sharp knife cutting slowly through leather. "But you want one of my girls. Is that it? You prefer fairer hair?"

Petrified, Will averted his gaze from Boulay's black, hypnotic eyes. He turned to Kate, who stood pressed against the wall at the bottom step, her eyelids clenched shut.

"Madame Boulay." Will heard his voice form the words, but he wasn't sure he was the one speaking them. "I meant no disrespect to you."

"Of course, you didn't." Sarcasm dripped from her full perfect lips. "Whenever men run from me, I take it as a compliment."

Will tried to regroup. "What I'm trying to say is—"

"Don't you think I'm beautiful?" she asked. She was now standing close to him, her lips just inches from his ear. "My skin, did you find a flaw?" Boulay stepped a circle around him. "Didn't you *want* to touch? Didn't you *want* a taste?"

Again, Will felt himself losing control of his body and mind. He felt Boulay's breath on his neck and the rustle of her dress against his legs. He pressed his eyes closed, and when he opened them again, he saw Kate, inching away from them.

"Madame Boulay," he said again, raising his volume. "Thank you for arranging a room for me, but I will no longer need accommodations. I will be settling my account with the sheriff." Will took a step away from the woman, holding tightly to the bundle of clothes. "Good evening."

Before he could turn to leave, Madame Boulay inhaled a deep breath, and Will imagined that he was being sucked into her lungs. "You cannot come into my place and order me around." Her slicing voice now seemed to be stabbing into him. "I will tell you when to come and when to go."

She reached out to touch him, but he sidestepped her hands. Joseph had told him not to let her touch him again.

"I will leave this place." Will looked around and saw the room starting to fill with others. He didn't want another scene like last night. He refused to run this time. "You're right, though. This is your place. It's all you." He lowered his tone and dared to lean an inch closer to her. "And one day, this place will be razed to the ground. Just like you."

Before she could take another breath or utter another word, Will rushed out through the door. He looked back for only a second and saw Kate running up the stairs.

Will wanted nothing more than to race away, but he already knew it was no use. He was tied to the Palace as long as Kate was there. No matter what Joseph had said, Will had to try to get her back.

He marched across the street to where Sam and Frenchie stood in front of the Enterprise.

"You didn't run. That is good," Frenchie said. He was whittling at the end of a stick. "She is not to be trifled with, but it is good that you let her see that you're not afraid."

Sam clucked and bobbed his head. "Oh, he's afraid, all right. But he's not a coward." Sam slapped Will on the shoulder. "I believe we all tremble in the shadow of the empress, but in our tremors, we take heart. For what giants have been slain with the smallest stones in the slings of the courageous. Whether fearless or with trembling, we must steel the path ahead."

Will shook his head. "I don't know about that. But I *am* going to kill her."

CHAPTER

FIFTEEN

Will, Sam, and Frenchie skirted the edge of town, coming to a run-down miner's shack just before sundown. Frenchie lit an oil lamp and made a grand gesture as the other two entered. "Welcome to my humble domicile. Sit, and we will eat as we talk."

"This place isn't far from my father's claim. I should go tomorrow and check on it." Will took a seat facing the door. "How long have you been living out here?"

"This little shack is nothing to the town. Nobody notices who comes and goes. I have been here for months. Nobody knows me. You two are the first people who have spoken to me since I have been in Virginia City. Besides the shopkeepers, of course. I buy bread and a few things for stew. I am a nameless miner, they think. Here today, but tomorrow gone. Looking for treasure wherever I may roam." Frenchie laughed. "If you want to share this place with me, you are welcome, Will. There are two beds."

Sam nodded to Will, taking the next chair. "You should accept the offer. All the rooms in town are controlled, one way or another, by Madame."

85

Frenchie spat toward the corner. "Elle-diable." He moved a bottle of whiskey and three tin cups to the table. "Will, I know that you want to kill her, but she is the reason I came to America. She is the woman I have hunted for the last several years."

Pouring out the drinks, Sam squinted as if in study, and his bushy brows helped to emphasize the expression. "Where did you follow Madame from, and why?"

After stoking a fire in the small stove, Frenchie moved a covered pot onto the heat. He lifted the lid and nodded. "There will be plenty," he whispered. Drawing up a chair with the others, he picked up his cup and sipped. "She murdered my wife and daughter. We had a home in Alsace. It wasn't much, but we had all we needed. Marie and my daughter, Anne, liked to pick berries in the garden at sunset. All summer they would find lovely things for our kitchen. One evening they didn't come back. I found them the next morning. Their bodies had been drained of blood."

Will leaned forward and sipped at his drink. "And what makes you think Boulay had anything to do with that?"

"She had been visiting them in the garden for weeks. Marie had shared some of the berries with her. She told me about her. Anne said that she looked like a queen." His face twisted with disgust at the memory. "She did it. Took them from me."

"It wasn't an animal?" Sam asked.

"They both looked as though they were sleeping. Like a fairy tale. An animal would have ripped them apart. I found them both lying among the berry bushes. On their left wrists was a bite. There wasn't another mark on either of them. I told the gendarme what I had seen. But like the sheriff here, he wouldn't hear a word against his precious lady, Juliette. Her name was not Boulay in France." He took another drink. "People had whispered about her for a while before it had happened. Animals had gone missing. Beggars were no longer on the streets. Rumors of witchcraft were everywhere for a time."

"Witchcraft?" Will and Sam asked together.

Frenchie nodded and continued. "The rumors were soon

replaced with compliments and honors. People in our village looked at her as if she was—like you said before, Sam—an empress."

Sam put his cup down and pulled out a pencil and a small note-book from his breast pocket. "You said you hunted her to Virginia City?"

Frenchie drained his cup and refilled it. "Yes. I followed her from France to New York. From New York to Charleston, to New Orleans, to Santa Fe, and then to Virginia City. Each place the same. First rumors of evil, then honors and praise. Each town a different name, but always the same woman."

Taking notes, Sam asked only a few more questions. "What does she do when she sees you in town?"

Frenchie laughed. "You think she might be worried? No. She has her followers. She controls them as she controlled my wife and daughter. They can see no wrong in her. They will gladly give their lives for her."

"I have a friend who said something about day-walkers," Will said. "Do you know anything about that?" He didn't want to try to explain about Joseph. No need to get him into more trouble than he finds for himself.

Frenchie dipped his chin and scratched at his blond whiskers. "That name, no, but it is the right term for them." He stood again, stirring the pot of stew and ladling it into three small bowls. He gave the other men each a bowl and spoon, keeping the last for himself."

Sam held up his pencil. "Now tell me about that. What is a day-walker?"

"They are the ones she has coerced into her fold. Her cult of devotees. They do whatever she wants or needs. She cannot move about in the daytime. The sun must be out of sight. This is why she prefers larger cities or places with mountains. She needs people who are under her control to do her bidding in the daylight." Frenchie nodded again. "Day-walker. Oui."

Will took a large bite of stew and thought about Kate as he

chewed. "Frenchie, do you know how one becomes a day-walker? How does she...?"

"I have not seen it happen, but I suspect things." Frenchie turned to Sam to interrupt his notetaking. "You should not represent this as fact."

"Understood." Sam licked the tip of his pencil and waited for Frenchie to continue.

"I believe she drinks their blood. I think about Marie. I think about little Anne." Tears glistened in his eyes as he spoke. "I believe she bites here." He pulled up his sleeve on his left wrist and pointed to the blue veins beneath the skin.

Will realized that he was sighing with relief when he saw no black cuff on Frenchie's arm. He quickly shifted his gaze to Sam's wrist. No cuff there, either. Another relief.

"With their blood in her body, she can somehow speak to their souls. She makes people do things. It is a deadly curse." Frenchie shook his head and spat toward the corner again.

"My friend thought that maybe the curse could be broken?" Will knew Joseph didn't believe this, but Frenchie didn't know that. He hoped it was possible, for Kate's sake.

Frenchie shoveled spoonful after spoonful into his mouth. "That I do not know, mon amie." He poured himself another drink. "I have only seen her leave a person in one of two conditions."

Sam poised his pencil for more notes.

"Dead—like my women, or undead—like herself. Once they become like her, they cannot stand the daylight." Frenchie waved his spoon at the others. "And listen closely, because I can tell you this for sure. When the day-walkers are found dead, one or two at first, then more—you will see that she is about to leave the city."

"Then we have to stop her here," Will said.

Frenchie waved a finger toward Sam. "He told me what she did to your parents. You will make a good partner for me. I have tried to kill her before. It is too much for one person."

Will nodded. "And Sam can help us, too."

Stopping mid-gulp, Sam raised his brow. "Will, they say the pen is mightier than the sword, but in this instance, I doubt a witch like Boulay will fear prose of pen. And I'm not one for wielding weapons."

Shaking his head, Frenchie coughed out an almost-laugh through a fume of whiskey. "Even a sword won't stop her." He gestured to a small pile of wooden sticks with ends whittled to a sharp point. "We'll need to put one of those through her heart. And through the hearts of the others she's made like her."

"But not the day-walkers?" Will asked urgently.

"I told you, I don't know about them." Frenchie sat back in his chair. "Here in America, you boast of your sophistication. Self-sufficient. You don't believe in the legends and myths. In the old country, monsters are real." He shook his head again. "They're real here, too. You just don't—or won't—see them."

Will hesitated. He wanted to tell them what Joseph and Ten Skies said. But most people didn't want to have anything to do with the natives. To the civilized of Virginia City, the Shoshone, or whatever tribes might be nearby, were no better than the monsters of legend. "I can see them," he finally admitted.

Sam finished his bowl of stew and nodded. "The monsters?"

"Yes, the monsters. I know how to identify the day-walkers. And, should I see any of Boulay's blood-sisters, I think I would know them, too." Will let it all spill out on the table. He would explain if they asked.

"Blood-sisters?" Frenchie rolled the words on his tongue. "How do you know so much about Boulay?"

"I have a friend." He hesitated to reveal too much.

"Who is this friend? He would make a good ally for us."

Taking a deep breath before responding, Will sat straight in his chair. "Joseph Dark Water is my friend. His uncle, Ten Skies, is the medicine man for the Shoshone settlement nearby." Will waited for them to gasp, but neither did. "They lifted a curse from me last night. Ten Skies gave me something to drink to see with his vision. He also poured oil over my head and shoulders to protect me from Boulay's influence. At least, I think it was oil."

Frenchie leaned forward and bobbed his head. "Can he do that for me, too?"

Blinking in surprise, Will shrugged. "I can ask him tomorrow. I will tell you that lifting the curse was not a pleasant ritual. I almost drowned."

Sam shook his head. "I hope neither of you will think less of me if I refrain from participating in a drowning ceremony."

"You are not a fighter, but you are a hunter of a different kind." Frenchie snickered. "You must tell this story whether we live or die."

Standing up and nodding to the others, Sam took a step toward the door. "I thank you for the delicious stew, Frenchie. And for the drink. I will excuse myself back into town and see you at sun-up, Will. I have an idea about poking around tonight for more information about Boulay."

Following him to the door, Will lowered his voice. "Just be careful, Sam. If you see anyone with a black band on their left wrist—they're day-walkers. Don't poke too much with them. And no matter what else happens, do not let Madame Boulay touch you. If you get a curse, we'll have to get it offa ya whether you like it or not."

"I understand." With that, Sam hurried out the door.

Will watched him disappear into the darkness. Turning back to Frenchie, Will sighed. "Joseph seemed to think that Boulay only turned other women into her kind. Blood-sisters. She doesn't turn men?"

Frenchie shrugged. "I have not seen her turn a man, but I think she could if she wanted to. I believe she lures men with the promise, but they never see the prize."

"What is the prize?" Will asked, returning to his seat.

"It is a true temptation." Frenchie picked up the bottle and swirled the golden-brown contents around the bottom. He poured first into Will's cup and then emptied the rest into his own. "You see, if she drinks your blood, she controls you. If she shares her blood in return, you enter into an unholy union—her sisterhood. She, and those like her, cannot be killed in flame or flood. Disease does not touch her. She fears neither a gun nor a knife. She cannot be drunk on wine, and she cannot be satisfied with food, gold, or love."

"Ten Skies said that as well."

"Her body will never grow old, and she will never die. That is her seduction and her promise. That is what she dangles before the eyes of her victims. Eternity and power, free from physical pain. For most, it is too much to resist." Frenchie drank his last gulp. "That is why I must kill her. I will be the man to pierce her heart."

Tipping his cup all the way back, Will finished his whiskey as well. "So that she can't break anyone else's." His hand brought down the tin cup hard on the table, and the bang startled both men.

"We should get some sleep. Morning will come earlier than we like." Frenchie gestured to the bed on the other side of the room. "You can sleep there. And I'd advise you to shake out the blanket before getting under. A bird was living here when I moved in. I think I got everything else cleaned out, but I didn't worry about that bed."

Half an hour later, the men were in their beds on opposite sides of the shack. Frenchie had turned the lamp off, but the heat of the stove still radiated out into the room.

Will yawned and sighed. "Frenchie, Ten Skies called Boulay a blood-sister. We've just been calling her a witch. What would she be called in France?"

"In the old country," Frenchie murmured, already dozing, "I must tell you, there are both men and women like her. In the bigger cities of France, it is like here. People don't acknowledge the monsters. But in the villages and small towns, people know. They know the name, and they whisper it in fear."

"And what is the name?" Will asked again.

Listening through the stillness of the night, Will heard Frenchie roll over in his bed and whisper through a sigh. "Vampire."

CHAPTER

SIXTEEN

W ill sat bolt upright in his narrow bed. The crow of a distant rooster or something else woke him up well before first light. He tip-toed outside to relieve himself and to see what had made the noise. Walking slowly around the shack, he saw nothing out of place in the purple glow of the coming sunrise.

As he opened the cabin door to go back in, he saw a flash of steel and heard the swift thunk of something on the inside door frame.

"Whoa," Will said. "It's just me."

Frenchie stood in the center of the room with his arm still extended from throwing his hunting knife. "Sorry. Pardon. I am not used to having a bunkmate. I forgot you were here."

Stepping back inside, Will extricated the knife from the doorpost and handed it back to his friend. "I understand. Better to be safe."

"Yes. But I could have hurt you. I will be more careful next time." Frenchie raked his long blond locks out of his face. "You are up early."

Yawning through a full body stretch, Will nodded. "I heard a sound. Maybe a rooster."

"Something close?"

Will shrugged. "I couldn't tell. I didn't see anything out there." He sat on his bed again and reached beneath for his boots. "I've got to get moving. I have to be at the paper before sunrise. What are you doing today?"

Frenchie yawned too. He tapped the flat of his blade against his shoulder. "I have to make a little money to buy some more food. My supplies are low again."

Getting dressed for the day, Will asked him, "I have a favor to ask. While you're out, keep your eyes open for a gray dapple horse. Sheriff Gregory took mine to the livery, but I don't know where he moved him after that. His name is Tiger."

"Why do you call a gray dapple Tiger? He has no stripes?"

"No stripes. It's more of an attitude than appearance." Will smoothed out his shirt and tucked the tails into his pants. "Tiger and I haven't been apart in years. I'm worried about him."

"You are right to worry, my friend. Good animals have to be watched." Frenchie pulled off his nightshirt and began dressing as well. "The sheriff cannot be trusted."

"Yeah, I'm finding that out." Will picked up his hat from the wall peg. "If you see him, just let me know where. I just want to make sure he's okay."

Nodding, Frenchie pulled his boots on and followed Will outside. "I will keep an eye out, as you say."

"See you around." Will tipped his hat to the man and headed back toward town.

Back in the city, Will looked from side to side, feeling as if someone was following him. But every time he stopped to check, there was nobody around him. The stillness of the morning faded as he neared the newspaper, and shopkeepers began their daily chores.

"Good morning," Will said to the man sweeping the steps in front of the general store. The man coughed and turned away without returning the greeting.

Will entered the front of the Enterprise just behind Jacobs. "Good morning, sir," Will said. Though his voice was low, Mr. Jacobs whirled around with his mouth agape.

"Shouldn't sneak up on a man like that, Bancroft." Jacobs shook his head. "Too early to be scaring folks."

"Yes, sir." Will left Jacobs and headed to the back room, stopping only for a moment at Sam's desk as he was sitting down. "Find anything with your poking around last night?"

Sam picked up a pencil and tapped his desktop for a moment. "Indeed, I did. And it concerns you, specifically. Jacobs will have me out at the ceremony tonight. Find me, and we can talk as I take notes."

"Can it wait that long? Should I make time earlier than that?"

"I don't think there's anything to be done earlier." Sam pursed his lips, making his mustache protrude. "If something changes, I'll ask Jacobs if you can assist me with another assignment."

Will lowered his chin half an inch and hurried to work in the print room. The press was already whirring in a quick, clipped rhythm.

Jack waved Will in while the other boys arrived and took their places at the tables. The stacks of papers soon grew taller, ready to be bundled and distributed.

As he had the last two days, Will brought the carts to the tables just as the first bundles were ready to load. The process got faster with each edition, and Will and the crew had everything ready to go out in an hour.

Jacobs had come in to ask one of the printers a question. He was about to yell, 'Back to work,' but then realized their morning work was done. "I suppose I should have hired someone to help months ago. I didn't know that one more pair of hands would make such a difference."

"Bancroft here has probably tripled our pace, sir," Jack said. "Not having to stop after each bundle to clear the table for the next one keeps us ripping along."

"Good job to all of you, then." Jacobs saluted all the boys and then turned to salute Will.

Will noticed that Jacobs kept his left hand behind his back and wondered if it was to hide the black cuff from Will's view. "Sir, if I may, when I'm out delivering the last round of papers, may I take a few minutes and check on a personal matter?" Will kept his posture straight and respectful. "It won't add ten minutes to my route."

Jacobs scowled for a second, then shrugged it off. "I suppose you've saved us more than that already today. But don't make it a habit. I can't let everyone run errands during business hours."

With a slight bow, Will said, "Yes, sir. And thank you sir."

Since he'd arrived and talked with Sam, Will had been wondering what Sam might have found that would pertain to him. He thought about what Gregory had said about settling his father's accounts. He thought about the silver mine.

And as he worked, an idea struck him. Will wondered about his father's claim. Sam had told him before that Madame Boulay had been telling folks that Victor was selling his claim to her. But something like that would have to be registered with a records clerk somewhere. Will was determined to see those records.

The morning passed quickly, and when it was time for him to deliver the extra papers to the stands, he was ready for his task.

He hurried to the Storey County Records Office and waited for a moment while a man in a brown suit finished a note in a ledger.

"May I help you, sir?" the man asked.

Will nodded politely and tried to check for a black cuff. Unfortunately, the man didn't raise his left hand above the desk.

"Yes, my name is William Bancroft, and I'm the son of Victor Bancroft," Will began.

The clerk bowed at the neck and placed his right hand over his heart as he stood. "I'm sorry for your loss. Victor was a friend of mine."

Will continued. "Thank you. I wanted to come in to check on my father's silver claim. I know where it's located. I worked it as a kid. But I wanted to make sure he hadn't sold it."

The clerk nodded. "Ah, you've heard the rumors, too. Yes, well, there was talk of your father transferring rights to Madame Boulay, but as far as our office is concerned, that transfer was never completed."

"I see," Will said. "And so, if money had actually exchanged hands, what would you need to make the transfer legal?"

"I would need to see a contract or receipt signed by both parties." The man straightened his jacket at the collar, and Will studied both wrists.

No black cuffs, but Will didn't let down his guard. "That would make it official?"

"Yes." The clerk nodded and sat back down at his desk. "And I'm very particular that all the signatures match."

Will held out his hand to shake. "I thank you for that."

The clerk hopped back to his feet to shake Will's hand. "And, Mr. Bancroft, I almost forgot. I have the death certificates for your parents, too. Will you need copies of those? I can have them for you tomorrow morning."

"Death certificates?" Will's heart thumped in his chest. He'd been so preoccupied with keeping himself safe and rescuing Kate from Boulay that he had let his parents' deaths slide to the back of his mind. Talk of their death certificates brought everything back. "Yes, I'll be back tomorrow for the copies. Thank you."

Will left the Records Office with a cloud over his head. His father hadn't sold the mining claim—but he knew that already. Now he just had to hope Boulay couldn't produce a signed document showing he had. Will didn't put it past her to try something like that. And he fully expected the law to back her up.

He'd have copies of their death certificates and nothing else. "Wait," he whispered to himself. Turning around to go back inside, he saw the clerk coming out.

"Mr. Bancroft, I needed to ask you something else. Would you happen to have any proof that you're Victor's son? I will need something before I can get you a copy."

Shoving his hands into his pockets, Will scrambled for ideas. "I think I can find something for you. And I had another question for you. My father's homestead is recorded here, too?"

"Oh, yes. I have that on file."

"And he didn't sell it, either?"

The clerk shook his head confidently. "No. And I know of no rumors about that at all."

"Thank you again. I'll be by tomorrow." Will waved, and the clerk returned to his office.

Feeling a notch more assured than before, Will grabbed the cart and headed back to the Enterprise. "Now I just need to find proof that I'm me." He realized that he was talking to Tiger, who wasn't there. "I sure miss you, buddy. But don't worry. I'm going to find you soon."

As he walked up the main street, he saw the sheriff and his deputies—he assumed they were deputies—putting up bunting on the porch rails and hitching posts. For the ceremony, he presumed. He had just a few hours until he'd be seeing the witch again. He spat on the ground at the thought.

"And if I do find proof that I'm me, I can get the death certificates. But even if I do, what will I do with them?" Will scratched at his chin, still talking to Tiger. "I don't have a place to put them, and I'm not getting a lockbox at the bank. The banker is one of hers. The only thing I will own—when I'm me—is a plot of land scorched to hell."

"I can probably find you a room in the sanitarium," Sam said as Will approached. "I'm not sure with whom you were speaking, but I suspect you lost them somewhere along your sojourn."

Laughing at himself, Will shook his head. "I'm used to talking to my horse. I guess it's taken his absence to realize I talk to myself a little too much."

"Nonsense," Sam replied. "I find it therapeutic to express my inner thoughts aloud on occasion. And sometimes, one simply needs expert advice."

"What did you need to tell me? What did you find out?" Will asked.

Sam motioned toward the front door of the Enterprise, and Jack hurried out to them and took the hand cart from Will.

"Thanks, Jack," Will said, releasing the handle.

"Happy to help." Jack nodded to the men and pulled the empty cart around to the back of the building.

"You're to be my assistant for the afternoon," Sam explained. "Jacobs was reluctant, but Jack assured him that he and the others could make it without you this one time."

"Like they always did before I was here." Will was eager for news. "You said you found something out for me. What is it?"

Sam raised his jaw to parallel with the street and walked toward the main square where the ceremony preparations were ongoing. "I think I found your horse."

CHAPTER
SEVENTEEN

The fine people of Virginia City were beginning to fill the streets and walkways along the route from the firehouse to the square. There was a hum in the air as the sun hovered low over the mountains. Most of the folks in town never saw the woman being honored—she never shopped in the stores or spent time in the parks. When she was out, it was in the evenings at parties or at the new opera house, or of course, at the Palace.

Men were anxious to see her on any occasion, in any state of dress. She was known by all to be the most beautiful woman in Nevada. Women wanted to see what they were up against and possibly glean some inspiration from how Madame dressed or wore her hair.

When women discussed Boulay's fee for her services, the first question asked was always, "What do you have to do for a thousand dollars?" The men were just as curious as to what an evening with the Madame might include.

As Sam and Will sauntered toward the newly erected stage, they heard every shade of conversation about the woman. Will's stomach turned just hearing her name repeated.

"Where did you find Tiger? Are we going to him?" asked Will.

Sam kept his pace without looking to one side or the other. "Patience, my friend. I'm not even one hundred percent sure it is Tiger. You said a dappled gray, and I haven't seen many of those in town. But I saw one this morning."

"Where?"

"You'll see. And I suppose you can properly identify your steed from other grays, correct?"

Will nodded with his whole body. "I definitely can identify him. He has six spots on his right rump that forms a star pattern. And he has a scar on the back of his left hind leg from where he got tangled in some barbed wire when he was still a foal."

Sam pointed to a bench at the corner of the square, close to the stage. "Let's take our places here. Close enough to see, but on the edge of the crowd just in case you need to make an expedited departure."

Following Sam to the bench, Will continued. "And he has a small rafter B brand just below the star pattern. I'll know him if I see him."

Pulling out his pencil and note pad, Sam gestured to the people assembling. "They all love a spectacle. They don't even care what it's all about. Half of them are curious about this woman of ill-repute, and the other half are frightened of her."

"I just don't understand why she has so much pull over folks." Will's head swiveled in every direction as he spoke.

"Do you believe Frenchie? Do you think she's some sort of witch or vampire?" Sam whispered.

Shrugging, Will murmured, "My friend Joseph thinks so. And his uncle." He felt a cool breeze on the back of his neck as he spoke. "I've never taken much stock in the ramblings of a medicine man, but he knew I had touched her just by looking at my hand."

"And he took a curse off you?"

Will nodded, thinking about the icy ritual. "And I don't want to have to do that again."

The sound of a trumpet blasted from down the street. A gang of young boys ran toward the square, yelling, "It's starting. It's starting."

Lines of people on the sidewalks leaned over draped railings and hitching posts to see the oncoming parade. Just as the sun dipped behind the mountain peaks, Will saw the beginnings of the procession.

Four men, presumably deputies, led the march by lighting the lanterns on the street and then around the square. Moths and other insects quickly swarmed around the lights. Though it was not nearly dark, there was no direct sunlight touching the town. A golden orange glow settled over the main street and square.

After the deputies, a man wearing a top hat and another man dressed in a black uniform marched solemnly down the center of the road.

"Who are they?" Will asked.

Sam scribbled a quick note. "The man in the uniform is Albert Sanderson. He's the Fire Chief in town. And Top Hat there is Mayor Runquist. He was the sheriff's puppet even before Boulay came to town."

Next came a troupe of six other men in uniforms.

Will waved a finger toward them. "And they're the fire brigade?"

Nodding again, Sam wrote a list of names for his article.

Scanning all the men as they assembled around the nearby stage, Will saw at least four of them had black cuffs around their left wrists. He was willing to wager that every man he saw was bought and paid for by Madame Boulay. He stretched his neck upward, straining to see who or what was coming next.

A cheerful rendition of "She'll Be Coming Around the Mountain" tolled out, performed by three men playing trumpets as they marched. Once they reached the square, they took seats in a row of chairs opposite the stage from Will's bench.

There was a long gap in the parade, causing the crowd to buzz in anticipation. Will and Sam both rose to their toes for a first look at what came next.

What they saw almost made them laugh. The bell from the church steeple had been mounted on a wagon. Three strong men pulled the wagon, while a young boy stood in the wagon, ringing the bell as if it were Christmas day.

"All this to celebrate a whore?" Will gasped.

Sam turned to him with a warning expression. In a low tone, he said, "I agree with you. You know that I do. But if you want the opportunity to dethrone this queen, you must keep your musings to a hush. Her sycophants are everywhere."

Tucking his chin to his chest, Will agreed. "Sorry. I just get queasy thinking about it all."

"I understand. But you have to be careful. You're the one with the most to lose."

And when he raised his head again, Will saw Kate's blonde hair. She, Carol Ann, and Redbeard were following the wagon with the bell, and behind them were four other women. Will assumed they were the other Palace prostitutes, based on their dress and how they teased the crowds as they walked.

All Will could think about was what his mother must have felt these last years, having to live in a town where sin was brazenly paraded down the street. She must have been sickened by all of it.

Will tried to catch Kate's eye, wanting to offer her a little hope. To let her know that she was not alone or forgotten. But she seemed to not see him at all. She looked past him without a blink or a nod. It was almost as if Kate's body was there, walking and smiling and waving to the crowds, but her soul was not. She was just an empty shell of the girl he used to know.

Sam poked Will's arm with the end of his pencil. "Look there, man."

Tearing his gaze from the woman he loved, Will redirected it back to the street. Approaching the square was the fire wagon, with its round water tank in the rear and ladders mounted on either side. Sitting on the driver's seat were Sheriff Gregory and Madame Boulay.

Pulling the bright red truck were three proud horses—a bay, a buck-skin, and a dapple gray.

Will's heart began pounding. The sounds of the crowd, the bell, and the trumpets faded. All he could hear was the slamming of his heart against his ribs and the clip-clopping of his horse.

"It's him," Will said through a gasp. "That's my horse."

"That's what I was afraid of," Sam replied. He continued writing. "I suppose we'll have to make a plan to retrieve him as well?"

"Yes, of course." Will's gaze followed his animal to the side of the stage. "We may need him to help us get Kate back."

Sam's head rocked back and forth, just a fraction of an inch. "Fantastic."

Sheriff Gregory and Mayor Runquist each took one of Juliette Boulay's gloved hands and helped her down from the wagon and up to the stage. She took her place next to Chief Sanderson. By this point, the people from the street had gathered around the square for the official ceremony.

Gregory began by calling for everyone's attention. "Good evening. I want to welcome all the fine folks of Virginia City to this ceremony. On behalf of the Mayor and myself, we thank you for turning out. It's good to know that the whole town supports our most prominent citizens."

Will watched Sam taking notes. He'd never seen anyone write so fast in all his life. He looked back at the stage, not wanting to look at Madame, but somehow unable to stop from staring at her. She was beautiful. Her black hair and eyes seemed to glow in the twilight.

"Stop it," he whispered to himself. He looked around at the crowd, and everyone—both men and women—seemed to stare the same way. Everyone was entranced by her.

He focused again on Tiger. He couldn't see the horse's right side from where he stood, but he could easily see the pale zig-zagged scar that ran up his left rear cannon from his hoof to his hock. He remem-bered the tears he'd shed as his father had carefully untangled the razor-sharp wire from around Tiger's leg.

"I'll get you back, boy," he muttered under his breath. "I can't stand that she has you, but at least now I know you're still alive."

The sheriff was still talking, but Will could barely hear any of it. He looked around the stage until he found where Kate stood on the far side of the platform.

He balled his fists as he thought about the life he had left her to. He thought he would be away for a year—two at most—to make a small fortune. He planned to come back, build a house, marry her, and start a family. It felt like everything went wrong from the start.

He spent all his money just getting to California. He had nothing to live on, let alone to purchase equipment for prospecting. He had to hire himself out for a year, just to find second-hand gear. And when he was on his own, he couldn't find anything but fool's gold. A fool was exactly the right word for him.

And knowing that while he was gone, Kate had lost her father and that the rest of her family moved away—it broke his heart. But to think that in her loneliness, Kate had turned to working for Juliette made him sick to his stomach. He couldn't leave her like this, no matter what Joseph said.

"I'll get you back, too." He didn't have to whisper this time because the crowd had begun to clap and cheer. He looked up to see Sanderson stepping forward and taking Juliette's hand.

"As you all know," Sanderson said. "Just a few days ago, Virginia City faced a blaze that threatened to consume our houses and our businesses. But with the help of this courageous woman, our little firehouse was able to stop the flames at our doorstep. And though we lost a few souls to that devilish wall of fire, we saved many, many more by Madame Boulay's delicate hand." He held up her hand in his to more cheering.

Will spat on the ground and looked around them to be sure nobody witnessed the insult. From the corner of his eye, he saw Frenchie in the crowd. The two men exchanged a nod and a grin. Will noticed a leather pouch strapped over Frenchie's torso. It was about the size of a cat, and Frenchie held his arm over it as though it was filled with gold.

He didn't have time to wonder what was inside it before Sanderson began again. "It is with great pleasure that I now name Madame Juliette Boulay Virginia City's Honorary Fire Chief."

Another burst of applause and cheering erupted as Sanderson pinned a badge onto Boulay's dress above her left breast.

"As always," Boulay said once the crowd quieted, "the pleasure is all mine."

Raucous laughter burst out in response.

Boulay smiled as she turned her head from side to side in a survey of her dominion. The crowd became nearly silent, waiting for more.

"I want to thank you all for this honor and for the esteem you have so generously bestowed upon me. I am proud to be a citizen of this fair city. I am proud to have you all as friends." As she spoke the word *friends*, her gaze landed on Will. He tried to look away but felt compelled to match her stare. "I hope that I can be as welcoming and generous to you as you all have been to me."

A warm sensation traveled out from his pounding heart, and a tingling spread down his arms and legs, through his nethers, and up to his cheeks. For a split-second, he felt complete lust for the woman, and his whole body showed it.

"Will, are you all right, friend?" Sam asked, jabbing him with his pencil.

The pain brought Will back to his senses. "I gotta move," he said and hurried from the bench around the back of the square to where Tiger and the other two horses were standing. Sam followed.

Reaching Tiger, Will began patting the horse's side. "Good boy," he whispered. He didn't want to draw any attention to himself as the madame's speech went on.

He pointed out the scar to Sam. "See here, just like I told you. A scar on his left rear leg."

Sam nodded. "Exactly as you said." Sam shifted to one side so that his shadow wasn't on Tiger's thigh. "And here are the spots that form the star. Also, as you said."

"This is Tiger, all right. I just have to figure how to get him back."

Will looked up to see Sam scratching his chin. "I only see one problem, Bancroft."

"What's that?"

"Where did you say your family brand was?" Sam shifted again, standing where more light fell on the horse.

"Well, it's right here under the star." Will stepped closer and pointed to the patch of gray thigh beneath the star. There was no brand in the horse's hide. Nothing.

"I don't see it," Sam said. He furrowed his substantial brow.

Will swallowed hard and smoothed his hand over Tiger's rump. "It was here. I swear. It was right here."

The horse snorted and swayed away from Will's touch. He stamped in the dirt and bobbed his head as though he was agitated.

Sam pulled Will away and into the shadow of the nearest building. "We need to get you away from this congregation. I sense that you're now in considerably more danger than we previously estimated."

Will looked up to see that Frenchie had joined them.

"Frenchie, take Will back to your cabin and keep him safe for the night," Sam ordered.

Agreeing, Frenchie took hold of Will's arm. "I can do that."

Standing frozen and befuddled, Will asked, "Why didn't Tiger know me? How could they turn him against me like that? What kind of person can do that?"

Sam shook his head. "I think the better question is what kind of person can make a horse's brand disappear?"

CHAPTER

EIGHTEEN

The sky turned a dark, purpled gray as Will and Frenchie approached the mining shack. Before they could enter, two shadowed figures stepped into the last light of day.

"Do not come closer," Frenchie warned as he drew his hunting knife from the sheath on his belt. "Who are you?"

In one swift move, the figures had Frenchie disarmed, and both men pinned against the cabin wall. "We do not want to hurt you," Ten Skies said in a low graveled growl. "You are making too much noise. Anyone can follow you." He sniffed at Will's breath. "You let her speak to you again."

Frenchie twisted his head toward Will, "I hope these men are your friends."

Will coughed. "They are. Joseph, Ten Skies, this is Frenchie. Can we please go inside?"

All four men relaxed slightly, and Joseph handed Frenchie his knife. "It's a good blade," he said. "You shouldn't let it be taken away so easily."

As Frenchie opened the door, Joseph scanned the area and then followed the others in.

Will offered the men the two chairs at the table as Frenchie locked the door and turned his attention to the stove.

"I found Tiger, but she has him—or the firehouse does. And he acted like he didn't know me." Will's voice poured out quickly. "And his brand is gone. How can someone do that?"

Joseph and Ten Skies exchanged a knowing glance.

"I told you," Frenchie responded. "She's a vampire."

"I don't know that name," Joseph said. "She is a demon of the air —a blood-sister with evil."

"Oui," Frenchie said. "It is the same." He looked Ten Skies and Joseph over and nodded. "You were quick to take my knife. I didn't see you coming. I need you to teach me that."

Joseph raised a brow. "You are hunting her for a long time?"

"Yes. I have followed her from my home in France. Many years now. Every time I think I am close, she moves on. Now I am here. I can see her. But she has an army with her. I think I need an army, too." Frenchie pulled some bread and a small bottle of wine from the bag across his chest. After setting the food on the table, he reached inside and pulled out a woman's stocking and a woman's handker-chief wrapped around a handful of tangled hair.

"What is all this?" Ten Skies asked.

"These are things I took from Madame's room. During the day, she is not in it. While the town was busy in preparation for the cere-mony, I sneaked into the Palace and stole them."

Will raised his brow in admiration. "That was daring."

"No. Not daring at all. I have been watching Juliette and her women. I only managed the courage to go in when I knew it was safe." Frenchie dipped his chin toward Ten Skies. "Will said that you gave him something for protection against her. Can you do the same for me?"

Ten Skies turned his gaze to the single, high window in the cabin. "The moon is darkening again. If you want to go through the ritual, I will do it tonight." Ten Skies stood and held his hands, palms down, over Frenchie's shoulders for a second, and then shifted one over his face and the other over his heart. "Yes, you have a strong mind and a right heart." He turned to face Will. "We will go when the moon is higher."

Sitting on the edge of his bunk, Will slumped. "I still don't understand. A brand can be changed but not removed."

Laughing, Joseph shook his head. "Will, you still believe you are fighting a woman. Boulay is not just a woman. She is a beast. Her powers are not human but spiritual. She uses flesh to satisfy flesh—and spirit to satisfy spirit."

Frenchie took the stolen items and set them out across the table. "I want to destroy both the flesh and the spirit." He gestured to his finds. "In the old country, they say you have to have the vampire's personal things, especially hair, to blind them from your plans."

Joseph crossed his arms over his chest. "This is good." He looked at his uncle. "Perhaps if we had these before, we might not have been stopped."

Ten Skies raised his shoulders and dropped them. It was less of a shrug and more of an acknowledgment. "What's done is done."

"You were with the raiders who took the girls and horses?" Will asked. "Why?"

His friend dropped his chin to his chest and released a long, labored sigh. As he raised his head again, Joseph's eyes looked dark and troubled. "Madame had made my Lily one of her day-walkers. I couldn't lose her to the Palace. I had warned her to stay away from Boulay, but she could not believe the stories I told her. She thought I was only trying to scare her."

Ten Skies furrowed his brow. "Lily thought I had filled his mind with legends of the old ways."

"Do not blame yourself," Joseph said. He turned back to Will. "Ten Skies told me to let her go, but I refused to believe she was lost. Some of my Shoshone friends joined me on a raid into town. We took Lily and three other girls and a few horses to carry them back to the camp."

Frenchie's face clouded. "I remember that night. You were all very brave."

"What happened?" Will asked.

"As soon as Lily saw us coming, she knew. And within a minute, Madame Boulay rushed out against us. The sheriff and his men were on us before we had made it out of town. Boulay shot two of us. I was only grazed," Joseph turned to show Will the scar on his arm. "but Chasing Crow was hit in the back. He died before he hit the ground. Four others were hit by Gregory and his men, and they were taken to jail. The next week they were hanged."

"I'm sorry, Joseph," Will said. "You loved Lily?"

"She was going to be my wife. Her father was against it, but she had planned to leave Virginia City with me." Joseph's tone took a sharper edge. "Even before the hangings, Boulay had made her a blood sister. It was Lily's testimony that sent my friends to the gallows."

Frenchie spat into the corner. "This is why Boulay must die. She kills for pleasure. She steals souls like it is a game."

"This is why," Joseph explained to Will, "you cannot just rescue Kate. She does not want to be rescued. If you try, Boulay will kill you."

Dropping to his cot, Frenchie nodded. "He is right. I try to remember that Boulay was once the victim of a beast, too. She was a girl like Kate, or Lily, or Marie, or Anne. She was consumed by a devil that turned her into a demon, too." He sighed. "But when I think about her appetite for blood, knowing it will never be satisfied." He dropped his head into his hands. "Knowing that my wife and daughter had to be buried with wooden stakes through their hearts, just to be sure." He began to sob. "I cannot leave her to take others."

Ten Skies jumped to his feet. "The moon is high. Come with us to the creek."

Joseph and Ten Skies led the way, and Frenchie and Will followed. When they reached the bend in the river, Joseph began building a fire, and Ten Skies reached his hands out to the others. "Take off your clothes."

Shaking his head, Will explained. "I already did this remove-the-curse thing. I don't need to do it again."

Frenchie nodded in agreement. "And I just wanted you to give me something to protect me from her."

Laughing, both Joseph and Ten Skies stayed on task.

"You must cleanse yourself of any curse or affliction she has assigned to you before I can give you protection." Ten Skies faced Will and scowled. "I gave you protection, but you allowed her to talk to you. She was close enough to breathe her poison onto your collar again."

"Well, what kind of protection doesn't even keep you safe from getting talked to and breathed on?" Will crossed his arms indignantly. "If I have to do this again, I want better protection."

Joseph nodded. "He has a point, Uncle."

Ten Skies squinted and expanded his chest in a deep breath. "Take off your clothes."

Frenchie crossed his arms, too. "I don't." He looked at Will. "Do we have to take off our clothes?"

Will exhaled and frowned as he began unbuttoning his shirt. "I don't like being naked. Not for something like this."

"Not really naked, though?" Frenchie asked.

Stripping off his boots, pants, socks, and underwear, Will growled as he left his clothes in a pile at Joseph's feet.

Frenchie huffed. "Oh, I see." And after a few more huffs, he pulled off his clothes as well.

Joseph took the clothing to the river's edge and nodded toward the pool. "You both need to get in."

Ten Skies tilted his head toward Joseph. "Take off your clothes, too."

"No, I don't need to. I haven't been cursed. I have all the protection I need."

"Are you going to help them?" Ten Skies asked. "They will need your help."

Joseph shook his head and then turned to Will and Frenchie. "Ugh." He took off his clothes and got into the water with the others. "I'm doing this because you are my friend."

Standing in the near-freezing water, the three men stared straight ahead at Ten Skies, who began his chant. After two verses of his recitation, he got down on his knees with the clothing and started dunking it all into the water. He continued his supplication as he dipped each piece and then held it up to the moonlight.

As he completed the process with each article of clothing, he took the cleansed item to the rocks around the glowing campfire. After the last piece, he knelt beside Joseph and pushed his head beneath the water. Then Joseph held down Will as Ten Skies drove Frenchie under.

The chanting began again as the men staggered out of the river and back to the fire, where they stood, quivering in the night while their clothes dried.

Ten Skies again opened his pouch and pulled out the contents. But this time, he mixed several liquids into one tin cup and set it in the coals for a few minutes.

"What is that?" Frenchie asked. A shudder rolled over his body.

Will blinked, stunned at the fact that he was once again standing naked beside a campfire. "It's our protection."

Gesturing to the cup, Ten Skies raised his face to the moon. "Your mission will require more than just protection. This drink will bind you three together. You will be strengthened. You will be alert. You will be protected. As long as you work together."

The medicine man picked up the cup and sniffed at it. He began another chant. Joseph checked the clothes closest to the fire and nodded. "They are dry enough."

The three men put on their underwear and shirts while waiting a little longer on their socks and pants.

Ten Skies held out the cup to Frenchie first. "Take a sip, then take a deep breath and release it slowly, then take one more sip." Holding the cup to Frenchie's lips, Ten Skies released a low, deep hum.

Frenchie took his sips and then stepped back. It was Joseph's turn. Sip-breath-sip, and then Ten Skies moved to Will. "You will do the same, but then you will finish the drink. Do not leave anything in the cup."

Will nodded, not understanding Ten Skies' reasoning. He took a sip of the hot drink, feeling it warm his mouth and throat. He took a deep breath, holding it for a second and then releasing it. It felt like fire in his lungs. He let Ten Skies pour the rest of the drink down his throat, not stopping until it was gone.

As he stepped away from the empty cup, Will's vision doubled for a moment and then focused in brilliant colors. "I don't feel cold now."

Joseph and Frenchie blinked. "I don't either," they said together.

Ten Skies held up his hands. "This will not keep you from dying," he said. "But it will help you to protect each other. You will have the vision to recognize evil. Even when it is disguised."

Before he realized what was happening, Will found himself and his friends sitting on the ground next to the fire. "I was hungry before. Before we came out here, I was hungry. But now I don't feel it."

Joseph leaned forward and grinned at the flames. "I have seen warriors drink this before. They are always happy afterward. Warm. Content. But it wears off."

Frenchie's head turned swiftly toward the city. "I think I can hear someone coming."

Ten Skies motioned to the clothes on the rocks as he extinguished the fire. "Get your things. I will take you back now."

The four men plodded to the cabin with their things tucked under their arms. Frenchie kept looking from side to side. "Will, do you hear it? Is there someone else out here?"

Will shook his head. "I don't think I hear anything. What does it sound like?"

Bringing up the rear, Joseph scanned in every direction. "I think I hear it. It sounds like an eagle flying."

Laughing, Will asked, "What sound does an eagle make when it flies?"

"Like that?" Joseph answered.

"But I don't hear anything."

But as the men approached the cabin, they saw a light inside, and a shadow fall over the window. They all froze in their tracks.

"Someone is inside," Frenchie whispered.

Ten Skies held out his hand to stop the others. "Silence."

Will wished he was wearing his pants rather than carrying them. He knew he was supposed to feel strong, but he couldn't remember feeling more vulnerable.

Frenchie pulled his knife from the sheath within the bundle in his hands.

"You won't need it," Ten Skies whispered.

Suddenly, the door to the shack flew open, and standing in the doorway was a silhouette of a man with wild hair.

"There you are!" Sam called out. "I brought food."

The men filed into the warm room, and Ten Skies took a seat at the table. Joseph, Will, and Frenchie went to different corners to pull their still-damp pants on, leaving their socks and boots by the door.

"What were you doing out there without your pants?" Sam asked.

Frenchie scowled. "We got our curses lifted and drank something to make us stronger."

"And no one drowned? That's grand." Sam opened a basket filled with roasted chicken, corn, and apples. He saluted Ten Skies and Joseph. "I apologize for assuming a dinner party of three, but I believe there are sufficient means for five, so long as none of us fall prey to over-indulgence."

Will smiled. "Ten Skies, Joseph, this is Sam. I work with him at the Territorial Enterprise. He's part of our team."

Before Ten Skies could make any suggestions, Joseph held up a hand to his uncle. "He doesn't need to go through the ritual. I can see he is pure of heart."

Sam grinned, and his mustache widened like bird wings. "I am pure of heart and fond of my trousers." He held out a hand to Joseph. "You're one of the raiders that escaped Boulay's bullets."

"Not unscathed, but still breathing." Joseph shook Sam's hand. "You're the reporter who writes with sympathy toward the Shoshone."

"Sympathy for all men until they give reason otherwise." Sam poured out a cup of wine and offered it to Ten Skies. "I'm delighted to meet you, sir."

Ten Skies took the cup and drank. He took the loaf of bread that Frenchie had offered earlier and broke off a piece, offering it to Sam. "I'm afraid after tonight, you won't be."

CHAPTER
NINETEEN

arrator's Aside Note:

Having heretofore avoided all ceremonies which required disrobing in the wilderness, I was the one man in our club of adventurers who could remain objective on matters concerning the preternatural. While Ten Skies, Joseph, and Frenchie spoke of monsters and curses, Will and I retained a healthy skepticism, though Will seemed to be losing ground with every hour.

I feel that at this point, I must remind you that while I was, on this evening, bogglish of the spiritual warfare in which I was entrenched, the battle was in no way lessened by my doubt. As an eyewitness, I can attest to all the strange diablerie unfolding before me. I may have been blinded to it for a time, but I soon came to know it as a real and tangible threat.

What's more, as I spent that evening listening to Frenchie and Ten Skies recount what a vampire or blood-sister or demon-of-air could do, I found myself wanting to know more. Hearing their accounts seemed to stoke a desire in me to see and experience the morbid and macabre. If I had known then what I know now, I might well have fled the city without farewell.

I stayed because I believed that I was to have a story to tell one way or another. As I write it, I realize my tale sounds fantastical. Again, I must reiterate that every word is true.

The most grotesque elements were still to come for our ensemble. And even if I had abandoned our quest—even if all the others had fallen away—young Bancroft would have stayed the course. His love for fair Kate was boundless. His love for his horse was almost so. To forsake the man in his time of need would have been unforgivable cruelty.

And so, our troupe spent that evening, and more to come, learning the foils of our enemy. We contended over strategies until we were of a similar mind. We discussed every contingency we could imagine, we thought, though we were naïve to what we were about to face. We believed we were prepared to slay the beast.

We were wrong.

CHAPTER

TWENTY

The men spent each hour of daylight watching the Palace, watching Boulay's day-walkers, watching for opportunities. They devoted each afternoon to finding felled branches and discarded wood scraps that could be sharpened into stakes.

In the evenings, Will and Sam listened to Frenchie and Joseph repeat the stories passed down through generations of their people. The hope was to find something to weaken the hold Boulay held over her underlings. The tales included ways to kill or die and ways to become a sycophant, but rarely did they contain anything about lessening the witch's power.

"One legend says that when the head beast is killed—staked through the heart—all those beneath them will be released from the curse." Frenchie whittled his stake to a fine, sharp point.

Joseph paused slicing at his stick. "Our stories are similar, but say that when the head of the viper is cut off, only the day-walkers can be healed. The other blood-sisters will continue in their deathless sleep." He held up his stake. "Are you sure this will work?"

Frenchie nodded. "Oui, yes. But it must penetrate the heart."

The stack of wooden stakes grew night after night, as did Will's determination. Sam took copious notes and, over the week, compiled them into a sort of primer for vampire-slaying.

While Frenchie seemed to know every detail about what had to be done to kill Boulay. Joseph was the expert on how to fight and kill with a stake. As Will and Frenchie learned the basic techniques, Sam would draw out the men's figures attacking each other, making notes about how and where to strike first to gain the advantage over an opponent.

On the night of the new moon, Ten Skies joined them at the cabin to perform a ritual over the items that Frenchie had stolen from Boulay.

"Let me see them again," he instructed. His voice was solemn. His face filled with intent.

Frenchie cleared the table of everything but the oil lamp before laying out the stocking and the linen square with hair.

Ten Skies cupped his palms and held them downward over each item. He started at the toe of the stocking and moved slowly to the other end. He kept both hands together over the hair, cupped at first, and then flexing his fingers outward.

"The hair has a significant portion of her spirit. The stocking has only a shadow of it. I will start with the hair." He pulled one shiny black strand loose from the tangle and held it over the oil lamp. When he lowered it closer to the flame, a green flash climbed up and consumed the hair, leaving nothing but an acrid odor in the room.

Will blinked in surprise. "I didn't know what I expected, but it wasn't that."

The medicine man took a small gourd from his pouch and shook it over the hair, creating a rattling sound. He began his canticle, punctuating it with hums and deep breathing. After several minutes he stopped and looked at the other men. "Let us see."

Ten Skies again pulled a hair from the tangle and lowered it to the flame. This time the hair disappeared into a puff of smoke and sickening smell, but no flash of green.

"You did it!" Will said, feeling a brief sense of relief. "What did you do?"

Laughing from one corner of his mouth, Ten Skies answered, "I removed Boulay's spirit from the hair."

Will looked at the other men's perplexed expressions. He wasn't sure how he was expected to respond, but only one thought pounded in his mind. "If you can take it from her own hair, then maybe you can remove her hold over Kate. Maybe even help Tiger, too?"

"Living, breathing things are quite different than a mass of hair, Will." Ten Skies shook his head. "I do not know how much of her spirit I expelled."

"But you said it was more than the stocking."

"Yes. The hair was once part of her body. The stocking never was."

Huffing with agitation, Will groaned. "Kate isn't part of her, either. Tiger isn't part of her body." He stood and paced to the window and back.

Ten Skies looked toward Joseph and dropped his head. "Their blood is alive within Juliette's body now."

Joseph put his hand on Will's shoulder. "She controls both of them."

Will dropped back to his seat on his cot. "I understand about Kate. I do. I didn't want to believe it, but I do now." He drew a breath and exhaled slowly. It came out in a nervous sputter. "But Tiger? She drank Tiger's blood? How do you know?"

Sam had his pencil poised for more notes. Frenchie leaned in to hear the man's explanation.

"You said he didn't seem to recognize you?"

"Right," Will said.

"At first, I was afraid she had made him one of her demons. I suspected that when I heard that his brand was gone. Boulay's blood can probably regenerate youth in her demons. I wouldn't have been surprised." Ten Skies sat down in the chair to be eye-level with Will.

"That is true," Frenchie said. "But I have never seen a vampire make an animal into one of their own."

Ten Skies continued. "But Joseph said that he saw the horse in the sunlight. A true demon-of-air cannot survive in daylight. They must spend their days in darkness."

Joseph raised his palms upward to his uncle. "Then why do we not find where they sleep and drive the stakes into them while they are unaware?"

"Wise. And if we had done that when Boulay first came to Virginia City, it would have worked, I believe." He gestured to the table. "That is why she has day-walkers. They can alert her to attacks. They will protect her at the cost of their lives."

"But animals, too?" Will asked.

"Our stories tell of using animals more often than humans. Animals do not get missed like people. No one sees an animal as a spy." Ten Skies held his hands up to the sky. "A demon-of-air can consume the blood of an animal—a raccoon or fox or wolf—and no one will think twice about it."

Will remembered the fox that had been in the tree as they were coming home. He thought about the way Ten Skies described vampires. "Why do your people call them demons-of-air?"

Joseph and Ten Skies looked at each other and then back to Will. Joseph sat straight in the chair by his uncle. "Our legends say that the demons can fly."

Frenchie slapped the table-top loudly. "I knew it!"

Sam blinked through an astonished expression. "You knew they could fly?" He touched his pen to his notepaper and then pulled it back. "I don't know if I should write that down or chuck the whole thing out the window."

Ten Skies gestured to the window for a second and then dropped his hands to his knees. "You do not believe. Most of my own people no longer believe these things. In another generation or two, no one will believe in anything." He leveled his index finger to each man around the room. "But you have seen things. And you will see more. Before you close your eyes for the last time, you will believe."

"I think I believe now," Will said. "When they fly, what do they look like?"

"Bats," Frenchie answered.

Ten Skies nodded. "They can take the form of a bat if that suits them. Or an owl, or vulture, or eagle."

"A vulture," Will murmured. "I saw one. Possibly. I don't know. It could have just been a vulture. Or it could have been Madame Boulay."

"Or one of her blood-sisters," Joseph added.

Sam hesitated for another minute, then shrugged and resumed his notetaking. "I suppose it won't detract from the rest of the narrative to include this minor possibility."

Ten Skies laughed. "Maybe I should tell you all of my stories. Maybe then people will believe."

Shaking his head and wearing a smirk, Sam replied, "Don't count on that. Nobody believes anything I say. And in most cases, it's for a good reason."

Will hopped back to his feet. "Even with all of this, the flying demons and cursed hair, and everything, I still have to fight. She murdered my parents. She's trying to take everything they worked for. And now she's stolen my horse and the woman I love."

Joseph shook his head, "Will, I know how you feel. I wish I didn't, but I do."

Before he could say another word, Will interrupted. "I know you do. And when you had the opportunity, you rode in and tried to rescue your love. All I want is the same chance."

"But it didn't work." Joseph's shoulder's slumped. "It didn't work, and people died."

Gesturing to the table, Will paced the floor of the shack. "But you saw what your uncle did." He looked at Sam and then Frenchie. "You both saw it."

Frenchie bobbed his head. "I saw. Puff of green smoke, verse and shaking, then puff of gray smoke. No more spirit."

"Exactly." Will whirled around to face Ten Skies. "You can take the spirit out of Kate. Out of Tiger. I believe."

Sam held up his pencil. "If Ten Skies believes he can, how do we make that happen? Joseph and Ten Skies can't just walk into Virginia City and start chanting and waving gourds over people. Not even over your horse. I feel confident that one of Madame Boulay's walker-people will put a stop to it before it begins."

Will looked around the room. "We'll bring Kate out here. I'll figure out a way to get her. It has to be during the day, of course. Sam, ask Jacobs for my assistance again, and we'll bring her out here." He turned back to the medicine man. "Or we'll bring her to the river if we have to. Yes, we'll have Ten Skies do all of it. The stream baptism, the clothes, the shaking, the drink stuff. Everything. I know it will work."

Ten Skies shot a doubtful look at Joseph and then stood. He turned to face all the men at once. "I will go now. And if you can find her, and if you can bring her to me at the river, I will try. Joseph, you will stay at the river with me. We will need help if the day walkers come after her."

Frenchie stood, too. "And I will be in town. I will find your Kate and let you know when she is out of the Palace. I'll get word through Sam."

Folding his notebook closed and tucking his pencil into his pocket, Sam got to his feet and stretched. "It appears that tomorrow will be a busy day. I should go home and get some rest." He saluted everyone, then shook Will's hand as he opened the door. "I'll see you in the morning."

"Tomorrow, we will make our first strike," Ten Skies said as he and Joseph left.

Frenchie waited for the others to leave and then gathered up Boulay's things and returned them to his leather pouch. "We will get your woman back," he assured Will. "If I had help like this in France, perhaps I would still have my women."

Will shook his hand. "We will avenge your wife and daughter soon."

Frenchie bent forward in a slight bow to Will. "Or we shall die trying."

CHAPTER

TWENTY-ONE

Will and Frenchie ambled into town with plans in place while the early morning sky still held the last stubborn stars in her rich velvet air. They parted ways a few blocks from the main street to prevent townsfolk from assuming an alliance.

Within seconds of their parting, however, Will began to feel the eyes of others on his shoulders. He took a casual turn, scanning the gray shadows in every direction. Nothing out of place. No one following. All was quiet except for the soft cooing of doves perched on the eaves and parapets of the shops on either side.

He eyed the birds suspiciously. Though they weren't vultures or owls, they were not above suspicion, now. Anyone could be watching him. Anything could be reporting back.

Taking the last dozen paces to the Enterprise more quickly, Will felt a rush of relief wash over him as he stepped inside. He hurried back to the press room, hoping to avoid running into Jacobs. He didn't want to speak to anyone who might give away his plan to Boulay.

The plan. Will needed it to work. For Kate's sake, it had to work.

Just after closing the print room door behind him, it opened again, and Jack joined the other boys at the tables.

"Good morning," the young man greeted everyone with a smile. "I heard another miner filed a lode claim. Out northwest. This town will be the richest city in the territory soon."

Will thought about his father's claim. He'd wanted to go out and explore the mine again to see how much it was really producing. But with Boulay's assertion that his father was deeding it to her, he didn't dare go out there and give her reason to call Sheriff Gregory. This would all be settled soon, anyway. That's what he kept telling himself.

"Sounds as though Sam will have another big article for today's afternoon edition," Will said.

"Probably so." Jack stacked his papers efficiently and began tying off his first bundle before the other boys were ready for their twine.

Working his way down the table and back, Will had the papers loaded and organized for pickup and then for delivery. He kept a close watch on the door, waiting for Sam to come in to collect him for assistance.

That was the sign that Kate was out of the Palace. That's when they would take her.

But Sam didn't come in.

It was time for the papers to go out, and Sam still hadn't come. Will was worried. Had the plan already been foiled? Was Kate spending the whole day inside the witch's fortress? Was she being forced to stay there? Will's mind conjured a thousand possibilities, all of them terrible. Will didn't like any of it.

"Time to deliver," Jack chirped as the last boy picked up his cart. "Will, do you need any help with the rounds?"

"I can manage," Will answered. He knew there was no black cuff up Jack's sleeve, but he was afraid of trusting anyone outside the main troupe. And he certainly didn't want a boy like Jack to be hurt by a beast like Boulay.

"I don't mind." Jack reached for the cart handle.

Will snapped it away from him. "I don't need help. You should stay here and be ready for the next edition. It will be out before you know it."

Jack's expression deflated. "All right," he mumbled. "I just wanted to help."

Guilt whipped through Will's thoughts. He didn't want to hurt his young friend. That's why he wanted him to stay. "Look, I'm sorry." His words didn't seem to cheer Jack, and he thought of another tactic. "I actually have a favor to ask. That's why I need you here."

With a slightly improved visage, Jack nodded, "Whatever you need, I can do it."

Will lowered his tone and put a hand on Jack's shoulder. "I may be delayed just a bit returning from my deliveries. Enough that Jacobs might notice." He hoped his words carried all the right implications for the youth's imagination.

"Say no more. I'm the man for the job. I have a dozen ways to keep him distracted." Jack seemed excited about the assignment.

"That will help more than you know," Will said. "I wasn't sure how I could make it otherwise."

"Don't worry about a thing." Jack saluted and returned to his station at the table.

Hesitating for a second while he shot a glance at the still-closed door to the reporters' office, Will saluted back and left with the loaded cart.

Out on the street, people bustled through their daily chores. Will tried to keep his gaze down and subdued as he walked past the Palace. No one stirred, either inside or outside the building. He knew Frenchie was posted somewhere nearby, watching for Kate, but Will couldn't see him, either.

He made his rounds and was almost back to the newspaper office when Sam strode out to meet him in the street. Like before, he gestured to Jack, who came out and took the cart from him.

"Another assignment," Sam said as Jack walked away from the

men. When the youth was out of hearing, Sam added. "Frenchie saw her go out the back a few minutes ago."

It was time to act.

Sam nodded ahead of them, where Will saw Frenchie leaning against a porch post on the next block. Using a cigar, Sam gestured to another man with a wide-brimmed hat pulled down low at his eyes. Will studied him for a second and then realized it was Joseph. Everyone was in position.

That's when Will saw Kate. She was dressed in a pale green day dress and a straw hat with a green ribbon tied neatly under her chin. She walked under the awning covers past one shop and then another. Her empty shopping basket swayed back and forth from the crook of her elbow.

Will watched her walk, thinking to himself that every time he saw her, he fell in love all over again. The idea of her being enslaved to a queen bee whore made his stomach turn. Kate was too pure, too lovely for that.

But as he watched his love walk ahead of him, he saw a glimpse of something else. A grayness followed her. Like an unholy shadow that clung too close, an evil ghost seemed to follow Kate. More than following her—it clutched at her clothing, her hair, her skin.

Ten Skies told Will he would be able to see evil. And whatever had hold of Kate was undoubtedly evil.

Hurrying his pace, Will was now just a few steps behind her. Sam and Joseph marched in line behind him.

"Kate," Will called, only slightly above a whisper.

Kate shook her head and continued walking.

"Kaitlin." Will raised his voice slightly but received the same non-response.

He had to keep trying. He didn't want to cause a scene or garner unwanted attention, but he was growing desperate.

Will doubled his pace and reached out for her, catching the edge of her shopping basket with his finger. "Kate!"

She whirled around with her eyes closed. She pressed her back to the side of the shop and shook her head from side to side. Her mouth formed the words, "please, no," but not a sound escaped her lips.

Dumbfounded, Will dropped his hand from her basket. He watched her as she shook her head and clasped her hands over her heart, and kept her eyes squeezed shut. He saw her reach into the little cotton purse that hung from her wrist and draw out a slip of paper.

"Kate, please," Will murmured.

Her anxiety became more pronounced as she threw the paper to the ground and ran away from him.

"Stop, please, Kate," he called out.

Sam and Joseph each took one of Will's arms to keep him from chasing after her as she disappeared around the next corner.

"You have to let her go," Joseph said.

Sam looked around them and lowered his chin and voice at the same time. "Too many people watching now. "Let her go. We'll have other chances."

"She dropped something," Will said, pulling free of Sam's grip. "Let me see what it is."

Will picked up the scrap of paper and unfolded it. Kate had written a note to him, but her handwriting was crooked, and the words ran together. He held it out where the other men could see.

"It appears that she wrote this missive either after imbibing too much strong drink or while she had her eyes closed." Sam took a step back to let Joseph examine the page. "And since she just ran from us with shaded eyes, I would guess that to be the case."

"She doesn't want Juliette to see what she wrote. She doesn't want her to see you, either Will." Joseph pushed the note back to Will's chest. "She still has enough of herself to warn you away."

"Come," Sam said, directing the others to a stack of barrels where they would be shielded from the eyes of others on the street. "We can regroup in private."

Will straightened the note in his hand and squinted through burning eyes to read Kate's message.

You must leave Virginia City right away. I wish I could go with you, but my fate is sealed. You have to let me go. You must find a new life for yourself. If you stay, you will be hurt, or worse. I loved you once. Always remember that. I want to love you still, but my heart has turned to stone, and I cannot love at all. I am lost. You must give me up, or you will be lost, too. That I could not bear. Please go.

A thousand knives cut through Will's heart as he read. He tried to look away from the paper, but his eyes were blurred with salty tears. "She says—" but he couldn't finish.

"I know," Sam said, patting Will on the shoulder. "We'll figure it out. She doesn't know our plan. She doesn't know we have a plan."

"For good reason," Joseph added.

"But we have to try." Will's voice choked. "We have to." Will's mind raced. He failed. Kate didn't want him to try again. But he couldn't leave her to the wicked hands of Boulay. He'd already done that. "Oh, what have I done? We can't fail again. We have to make it work, no matter what the cost. Kate's in more danger now than before."

Joseph and Sam exchanged a glance, and then Sam left the men and crossed the street.

"Where is he going?" Will asked.

Joseph inhaled a deep breath and leveled his gaze with Will's. "We failed at this part of the plan, yes. But there still may be hope for your horse. Sam and Frenchie will do their part. We have to be fast, and we cannot fail this time."

"We thought we couldn't fail with Kate." Will swallowed hard, not wanting to even think about what might happen to his love. "She wouldn't even talk to me."

"She did not want to put you in danger. What's left of her loves you. You have to hold on to that." Joseph frowned. "Lily did not even have that for me."

"If we fail again with her, Juliette will make her a blood-sister, or worse. She could kill her." Will tasted the bile rising in his throat as he said the words.

"Death is the kinder of the two—for her."

Will folded the note and slipped it into his shirt pocket. "We can't fail her again." He looked up the street, where he saw a billow of smoke just above the top of the next building.

Joseph motioned ahead of them, as a man on the corner began to yell, "Fire! Fire!"

Will scanned the area as they hurried toward the smoke. "It looks like the fire is at the firehouse," he said. "We have to hurry. Tiger is in there. We have to get him out."

"That is the plan," Joseph reminded him.

"And we can't fail him, either" Will gasped as his trot became a full-speed sprint.

Joseph ran beside him. "If we do, we'll be dead by dawn."

CHAPTER

TWENTY-TWO

As Will and Joseph approached the firehouse stables, a crowd was already forming around the small building. Sam was standing at the stable doors, yelling to others for help.

"We have to get the horses out! The whole thing could go up in minutes!" Sam cried at the top of his lungs.

Frenchie came from behind the stables carrying handfuls of dark cloth. "I have some hoods for them. Who will help me get the horses out?"

Will lunged forward, desperate to reach Tiger. Joseph held him back. "Stay here. Frenchie will bring him out, and then we will have to leave quickly. Let the crowd get the other horses."

"But I don't want any of the horses to perish," Will insisted.

Joseph shook his head. "None will be hurt. There is much more smoke than fire. And it is not where the animals are kept. Come with me to the side."

Will followed his friend, watching Frenchie and four or five other men rush into the stables. Smoke flowed out for another tense minute as the crowd grew thicker. Sanderson arrived just a minute later and took control of the situation.

"Men, get the pumper truck out here. Let's find the source and douse it." He waved his arms to direct his men and held up his hands to the wall of people in front of him. "Ladies and gentlemen, stay well away. My men have this under control. I don't want anyone hurt."

In another minute, a man exited the stable with a horse wearing one of the hoods. Several in the crowd began to cheer. Next came Frenchie, leading Tiger, also hooded, followed quickly by two more men and two more horses.

As the people applauded, Sam yelled again. "Stand back! It looks like the fire is spreading!"

"We have to hurry," Joseph said, pulling Will with him.

The assembly scattered in every direction, and amid the chaos, the men joined Frenchie and Tiger as they hurried away from the firehouse. They left Sam to manage the scene.

Will and Frenchie led the still-hooded horse out toward the creek where Ten Skies waited. They didn't dare to remove the black cloth from Tiger's eyes for fear he would revolt.

Reaching the bank of the stream, Will finally began to feel hopeful. They had managed to avoid being stopped in town, all the while keeping Tiger under control. This was going to work.

Ten Skies met them at a deeper portion in the river and gestured for them to bring the horse into the water.

Nodding, Will used his series of tongue-clicks and one-syllable commands to coax the horse into the current.

"Now, keep him still if you can." The medicine man waded into the water with his gourd-shaker in one hand and a clay pitcher in the other. He started his chant slowly, moving the gourd softly up and down in rhythm with his song, shaking it just above Tiger's neck and back.

When he had worked his way from his head to his rump and all the way back, Ten Skies stopped shaking the gourd and began to pour out the liquid from the pitcher over Tiger's mane, back, and tail. He rubbed it in and gestured for Will to do the same.

Without missing a word of his chant, Ten Skies nodded to Joseph, who was still standing on the bank. Joseph picked up a burlap sack from a nearby rock and carried it into the water beside his uncle. Standing near Tiger's nose, Joseph handed the bag to Ten Skies and ripped the end of the hood open.

"Whoa, boy," Will whispered when the ripping sound caused the horse to skitter.

Ten Skies continued his chant as he lowered the sack to Tiger's mouth. The horse sniffed at it, then pushed his nose inside the bag and began to munch.

Will continued to rub the liquid into Tiger's coat, remembering all the times he'd brushed out burrs and untangled his mane. He could feel the muscles in Tiger's neck flex and relax as he chewed. The feed's sweet smell had a different aroma than what Will remembered, but he assumed it was whatever concoction Ten Skies had mixed to banish the curse.

Everything was going to be okay. Will would soon have Tiger back. "Good boy," he heard himself saying out loud.

But at the sound of Will's voice, Tiger reared up on his hind legs and snorted. His front hoofs cycled in the air, missing Ten Skies and Joseph by only inches. The men backed away, trying to calm the horse again.

Will raised his hands over his head and stepped back. With tears in his eyes, he watched Tiger shake his head free of the hood and bolt up the bank. Tiger again reared up and kicked Frenchie in the side, sending him flat on his back.

Once out of the water, Ten Skies bent down to help Frenchie, who gestured for him toward the horse. "I am well. He only knocked the breath out of me. Help him."

Will and Joseph tried to calm Tiger with soft words and low hand-motions, but the horse only grew more agitated.

"Uncle," Joseph muttered. "Is there not something to calm him?"

"Only what was in the bag."

"Tiger," Will pleaded with the horse. "You know me. We're friends. Please, let us help you."

Tiger's head bobbed and shook in a fury. He pawed and stomped and kicked as if he had never been broken. He reared and charged at both Will and Joseph. Tiger's snorts turned into shrieking neighs, and his eyes glazed in terror.

"It's all right, boy," Will said. His tone was calm, though every muscle in his body shook with fear. "You're going to be all right." He took one cautious step and then another. He held out his hands low and wide, nodding his head toward Joseph, signaling that he could step back.

Tiger's stance seemed to soften. He lowered his head and released a long slow chuff. He stopped pawing at the dirt and tossed his mane as though he were shooing away a fly.

Will exhaled a sigh of relief and took a more relaxed step toward his old friend.

Without warning, Tiger charged Will with the force of a devil, knocking him on his back and trampling over him before racing away toward town.

Will stared up at the sky for a few seconds. The pain in his crushed body was nothing compared to the searing fire in his heart.

"I've failed again," he mumbled as everything around him turned black.

CHAPTER

TWENTY-THREE

"We need to find a place to hide him."

Will wasn't sure who spoke the words but felt certain they were talking about him. He tried to open his eyes and managed a slit of light on both sides. He looked from side to side without moving his head. Joseph, Frenchie, and Sam were all standing around him. He thought he could hear Ten Skies chanting nearby.

"You think it is bad to take him to the shack?" Frenchie asked.

Sam answered. "Whatever you do, don't take him back to the shack. She will be searching every outbuilding she can find. Sanderson and Gregory were already looking for the horse before he came back to the firehouse. I'm confident they suspect Bancroft reclaimed him."

"What about where you are staying?" Joseph asked.

"My landlord pries into everyone's business. And he wears a black cuff." Sam raised his left hand, gesturing to his wrist. "What about you, Joseph? Is there a sanctuary at your settlement?"

Joseph dropped his chin to his chest and frowned. "After my

brothers were hanged, the elders refuse to have any white man on our ground."

The chanting stopped, and Ten Skies joined the others. "We should take him underground. Someplace unseen from the air."

Frenchie raised his brow. "What about his father's mine?"

"She may look there as well. I'd wager she'll have all the black cuffs in town scouring every inch of the county until she finds him."

"I still don't understand what she has against my family." Will's voice choked out, startling the others.

"You're awake." Joseph's serious tone broke for a second. "Can you move?"

For the first time, Will realized he was still sprawled out on the ground. "Of course, I can move." He tried to sit up, but every muscle in his body ached. "I'll move in a minute."

"We cannot stay out here like this. The sun will be down soon." Ten Skies began checking Will for broken bones. "Is there a root cellar somewhere? Or something like that?"

"All the buildings I know of with any type of cellar are owned or managed by a black cuff." Sam shrugged. "She'd know where he was by noon."

"Mother insisted," Will groaned.

Frenchie bent closer to hear. "What did you say, Will?"

Struggling to get his elbows in position, Will propped his upper half up to face the men. "My mother insisted that she have a root cellar under our house. My father built one for her. It was under the kitchen. If the house didn't collapse into it, we could go there."

Joseph shook his head. "Frenchie, you help me get Will to his homestead. Sam, go back to town. Send word if you hear anything." He scanned the banks of the river in both directions. "Uncle, go ahead of us to the remains of the house. Make sure the cellar is not barricaded. Say your chants until we arrive. We will come at the fastest pace Will can manage."

Ten Skies nodded and disappeared toward the family homestead. Sam carefully placed a hand on Will's shoulder. "Don't worry about coming in tomorrow morning; Jack and I will take care of Jacobs for you."

"Thanks, Sam."

"I'll check in tomorrow afternoon for my next assignment." Sam grimaced and then got to his feet and hurried back to town.

Frenchie and Joseph got on either side of Will and raised him to his feet. Taking short, pained breaths, Will took one careful step and then another. Every move was agonizing. His bones didn't seem broken, but everything felt bruised and battered.

"We have to move faster," Frenchie said. He pulled Will's left arm across his shoulders, and Joseph did the same with Will's right. Together, the three men raced up the hill toward the blackened plot of land where the bones of Will's former home languished.

As they passed the gravesites of Will's parents, Frenchie paused for a split second to cross himself. "May they rest in peace," he whispered.

Ahead, they saw Ten Skies with his arms stretched to the rising moon. He was repeating a new chant, with longer, deeper hums between sharp rasps. When they were at his side, he reached down and pulled a scorched trap door open. "When you are inside, I will cover the top with dirt. It will be invisible from above."

Joseph led the way, and Frenchie helped to steady Will on the steep ladder-like stair steps into the hole.

"Mother kept two lanterns down here if they didn't burn up in the fire."

The last fingers of dusk grazed the cellar opening, and Joseph took a moment to scan the small room. "I see one."

A minute later, he had the first lantern glowing and had found the second. "I will have to go with my uncle, but I will be back in the morning."

"No," Ten Skies said. "You should stay with your friend. He may need you." And without another word, the medicine man dropped the trap door closed.

"Let's see what we have in here," Joseph said.

One wall was lined with shelves filled with canning jars of every vegetable and jelly Will had ever tasted. Working clockwise, the next wall was stacked with crates, large and small. The next wall supported the stairs, but below the stairs were a stack of three long, flat boxes.

"Those have long guns in them," Will said. "I can't believe everything down here is untouched by the fire."

Along the last wall were bins of potatoes, carrots, and onions, all smelling of rich, dark earth. In the center of the room was a small table with a three-legged stool underneath. It was where Will's mother sat to organize her canned goods or sort through the veggies.

It was where his father sat to reload his shotgun shells or to clean his guns. They had been here, at that table just a few weeks ago. They didn't know then what was coming.

Will pointed to the largest crate. "There should be blankets in there." He looked at one of the smaller ones with rope handles on either end. "Mother kept wine in that one."

Frenchie laughed and then clasped at his side where Tiger had kicked him. "Your mother is still taking care of you. She must have been a wonderful woman."

"She was," Will said. "I should have been a better son to her."

"We should all be better sons to our mothers," Frenchie added. He pulled the stool clear of the table and lowered Will onto it. "Let us make a home of this place."

Joseph and Frenchie worked for a few minutes to make pallets for them on the floor. Joseph found more oil for the extra lamp, but they decided not to light it yet.

"We don't know how long we will be here." Joseph shifted the boxes around to make a bench for more seating at the table. "What is in this one?" he asked.

Will studied the box and shrugged. "I don't think I've seen that one before. Let's open it up. Maybe it's got some fresh clothes. I smell like I got trampled by a horse."

Pulling the box over to catch more lamplight, Joseph tugged at the top. "It has a lock."

"Look under the top step of the stairs. There should be a hook with keys on it." Will pointed to the underside of the tread.

Joseph reached up and found a key ring with three keys. "Right where they are supposed to be."

Glancing around the room, Will sighed. "Mother liked to have everything in its place."

Trying the first key, Joseph shook his head. "Too big." He held the others up to the light. "This one." And the second key slipped perfectly into the keyhole and clicked. Joseph lifted the lid of the box, and all three men released a gasp at the same time.

Sitting atop a large leather wallet was a small, glistening gold bar and two pearl-handled revolvers. Tucked to the side of the wallet was a leather belt wrapped around a pair of holsters. Beneath the wallet was a photo in a gilded frame.

"What is all that?" Will asked. He leaned forward to see, ignoring the stabbing sensation in his ribs. "I don't remember my father having any kind of rig like that."

"Maybe he didn't need it until recently?" Frenchie surmised. "He realized what he was up against. Or he thought he did."

Joseph pulled the wallet out and handed it to Will. "You should be the one to open this."

Will loosened the leather cording that held the wallet closed. He unfolded one side and then the other. The leather was still new and stiff. Within the wallet, Will found several pages of documents. Holding them up to the lamp, he could see that they were all legal papers with fancy lettering and large, looped signatures and seals at the bottom.

"This first one is their homestead registration." He flipped to the next. "And the silver claim, and the deed to their mine." Tears burned behind his eyes as he tried to focus. "My father took everything out of the bank and brought it here. He was scared." He carefully wrapped the wallet back up and secured it again. "What's underneath?"

Joseph handed him the framed picture. Will studied the grainy image, fighting the urge to let go and scream. He remembered the afternoon of the portrait. His mother insisted that he and his father dress in ties and vests, and she wore the pale blue dress with ribbon at the collar. They stood completely still in the overheated parlor for what seemed like an eternity while the photographer fiddled with the camera contraption.

But when the picture was delivered, Mother had been more pleased than Will had ever seen her. It was her prized possession. And now it was in a box in her root cellar.

As if Frenchie had known what Will had been thinking, he said, "She was keeping it safe. Perhaps she did know."

"The box is full of all the things they wanted to protect. Everything they wanted to keep out of Madame Boulay's claws," Joseph said. He pulled a family Bible from the box and gasped when he saw what was underneath. "I know why this crate was so heavy." He set a large pouch on the table next to the gold bar. And then another, and another.

"What is inside them?" Will asked.

Frenchie smiled. "Can you not smell it? My friend, the bags are full of silver."

Will loosened the drawstring on the first bag, and inside he found several dozen small ingots of shiny silver. "I never dreamed he'd found this much."

Joseph looked at the table and then back to the box. "This is all the reason Boulay needed to go after your parents. And by all accounts, she has no idea this is down here."

Will shook his head and handed the things back for Joseph to replace. His pain was entirely forgotten. "I had no idea it was down here."

Frenchie shot a grave look at Will. "Killing your parents didn't get her what she wanted. But killing you will."

CHAPTER
TWENTY-FOUR

"Then all that's left is the killing or the dying." Will sat up after a fitful night's sleep in his makeshift bed, sharpening a scrap of wood from his father's kindling pile.

Joseph had wrapped Will's ribcage with a length of cheesecloth from the canning supplies. Frenchie whittled his own stake while Joseph cleaned the shotguns.

"Who knows what we will need against the devil?" Joseph muttered. "But we should be ready."

Frenchie saluted, tipping his knife toward Joseph. "The guns and blades may slow her down, but only the spear will kill her."

"And why are we not going to find her as she sleeps during the day?" Joseph asked. "She will not be able to fight us."

"I have tried this before. But Juliette's day-walkers are on high alert while she sleeps. They are her eyes and hands and feet." Frenchie gestured to the guns with his knife. "They are her sacrificial lambs and her weapons all in one. And they are her victims, too. It is best if we harm only those absolutely necessary."

Will sniffed and stretched his sore arms. "And Sheriff Gregory. He's gotta go."

"I agree." Joseph finished with one gun and picked up the next one. "Some of the others may not understand what Boulay is or does, but I am sure he knows."

"You are right, friend," Frenchie said. "Since I have been in Virginia City, he has been saying that Madame Boulay offers eternal life. He talks about it more than the preacher at the church. Such sacrilege cannot go unanswered." He spat toward the corner.

"What is our plan, then?" Will asked. "If we go into town tonight, won't she be more protected? The day-walkers will see us, and she'll be ready for us with all her strength."

"Ahh, one would think," Frenchie said. "But I have found that at night, most of her day-walkers are resting in their homes. Only the ones in the Palace will be watching. And she will think she has the advantage of her fortress to stop us. She will be over-confident."

"But we still must be on our guard," Joseph said. "She will be fully capable of taking all of us in a matter of minutes. Then it will be her choice to kill or use us."

"Exactly," Frenchie said with an edge to his tone. "One bite will enslave you." He turned to face Will and then Joseph, making eye contact for emphasis. "If she bites me, do not let me live. Do you understand? I would rather go to the grave than to be one of her day-walkers. And do not just shoot me, either. I beg you to put a stake through my heart, too. After years of hunting this demon, I will not let her damn my soul to eternal fire."

Will shuddered at the thought of what they all faced. The idea of fighting a beast like Juliette Boulay made his gut ache. She was a murderer of the worst kind. She wore her sin—every sin in the Bible—like a crown on her head. She was the very bride of Satan, Will thought. And it was his job to defeat her.

"So we go to the Palace?" Will asked. "Right through the front door?"

Shaking his head, Frenchie answered. "No, we will go up the back stairs. We wait until we know Boulay is in her room, and then we strike." He took a deep breath. "With all three of us, perhaps we have a chance."

Joseph cleared his throat and focused on oiling the gun in his hand. "And the blood-sisters? What do we do about them? They must die, too. If we let any of them live, they will take Madame's place."

Will knew that Joseph was thinking about Lily. He had nearly died trying to rescue her once. Will considered for a moment if she was past saving. "Maybe once Boulay is dead, the blood-sisters will be released from the curse."

"No," both Frenchie and Joseph said together.

"Unfortunately, a fully-transformed vampire cannot be redeemed." Frenchie continued, "They have given themselves over to evil and consummated the union."

Joseph dipped his chin in agreement. "Our stories say the same. Their souls are lost to this world."

"I'm sorry, Joseph." Will shifted toward his friend. "I wish you did not have to suffer this way. This will be difficult for you."

"We have all lost our hearts to this woman." Joseph motioned to Frenchie. "He lost his wife and daughter. You have lost your parents, Tiger, and Kate." He cleared his throat again. "I have lost Lily and my brothers." His voice became weak and trailed off.

Frenchie forced a resolute nod. "We must stop her before she takes anyone else."

The three men spent the rest of the day sharpening stakes and eating carrots and pickled eggs. Frenchie checked his pocket watch several times each hour.

"We should prepare ourselves for the fight ahead." Frenchie paced the floor. "I will pray for our success." He looked at Joseph. "You should, too."

Will stood and stretched, trying to loosen his aching muscles. Hoof-shaped bruises rose over his chest and shoulders in dark purple and blue. Red scuffs and abrasions covered his shoulders.

He picked up the photograph of his family from years ago and looked at his mother's sweet face. She didn't deserve to die so young. Not for the greed of a witch. He studied his father's stern expression. This was the face he always remembered. Not angry, but never quite pleased. He constantly strove to do more—to be better. Never content with life as it was.

Will couldn't remember his father laughing or even smiling. He tried to imagine it. He hoped that they had moments of joy together before the end came. He prayed for that.

Looking up from the picture, he saw Joseph with his face turned upward and his eyes closed. His lips were pressed into a thin, straight line. He knew that Joseph didn't pray like the Christians of Virginia City or the Shoshone's elder tribesmen. He was caught somewhere between the two—an abomination and disgrace to both.

Using the three-legged stool as an altar in the corner of the room, Frenchie knelt with his hands clasped together. He mumbled a prayer punctuated with moans and sobs.

Will wondered how old the Frenchman was. When they first met him at the Palace bar, he had guessed he was a dozen years older than himself. Maybe in his late thirties. But now, as he listened to the man pray and cry, Will guessed that Frenchie was probably in his fifties, closer to his father's age. He wondered how many years he'd been hunting Boulay. He wondered what life he had lived before his family was stolen from him.

Was he a farmer? Was he a tailor or a barrel cooper? As Will watched him pray, seeing him kiss the silver cross he wore on a chain around his neck, he wondered if he had been a clergyman. Will listened closely. He didn't understand Frenchie's words, but he felt the emotion all the way through to his marrow. In the short time that he had known the man, Will had seen him laugh and weep. He took comfort in that thought.

As he finished his prayer, Frenchie crossed himself and stood. He pushed his long blond hair away from his face, and Will could see his red-rimmed eyes, full of determination.

Pulling his torn shirt over his bound chest, Will took several deep breaths, releasing them slowly, hoping the pain would lessen with each one.

All three men pulled on their boots and found pouches for their stakes. Joseph strapped on the holster rigging and the two revolvers as well. Frenchie slipped his knife into the sheath on his belt. Will scanned the cellar for another weapon he could take with him other than the shotguns. He needed to keep his hands as free as possible.

On the shelf beside his father's gun boxes, he saw his father's boot knife. It was small, but it was better than nothing. He took the small leather pouch and slid it into his boot, tucking it—handle up—into his sock, just behind his right ankle. He hoped he wouldn't need it, but he felt better knowing it was there.

"Once we leave this cellar, we will be vulnerable." Frenchie patted the stairway. "We should keep to the quiet streets until we are close to the Palace."

Will nodded. "And what do we do if we get separated or if things go bad? Should we decide on a place to meet and regroup?"

Joseph and Frenchie exchanged a worried glance.

"We will not have another chance after this, said Joseph. "When we leave here, we go to war,:

Frenchie added, "We will either win or die."

CHAPTER

TWENTY-FIVE

As the men reached the edge of town, Joseph directed them toward a secondary street to take them to the Palace's back stairs. The homes were already quiet for the night, with lamps burning upstairs instead of down.

The moon was split in two, with one half a brilliant white and the other black with a hint of a blue-shadowed edge.

"I feel as though someone is following us," Will whispered to the others. "I've felt it all week." He made a full turn as he walked, seeing nothing out of place. He paused for a few seconds to scan the sky. "I don't see any birds or bats."

Frenchie shrugged. "Keep watch. If there is someone behind us, we may not know until it is too late to run."

They walked another block, but the sensation remained. Will swiveled his head back and forth, looking for any movement out of place. He saw nothing.

Joseph and Frenchie walked on either side of Will, and the group's formation tightened the closer they got to the saloon. At the next intersection of streets, Will was sure he heard another set of footfalls.

He stopped, motioning for the others to pause, too. That's when they heard it, also. Footsteps plodded toward them.

Joseph listened closely, stepping out in front and drawing one of his pistols. He cocked the hammer and leveled the barrel toward the shadow approaching.

"Whoa, there. It's me," Sam murmured. "I've been watching for you since sundown."

Joseph lowered his shoulders as he carefully uncocked the pistol. "I could have shot you."

Sam's brows raised and lowered with the tone of his voice. "I wasn't sure what you would need me to do. I have a small pistol." He held out a little Derringer, catching the gleam from the moon. "I know I'm just a wordsmith, but I want to help."

Joseph grinned at Sam's weapon, and Frenchie nodded.

Will gestured for him to join them. "Come on, then. We're on our way to meet our fates."

"Yes, well," Sam began. "I will do whatever you ask, of course. But I would like the chance to write about it afterward."

"We'll do our best," Will said with grim determination.

They walked on until they could see the lights and hear the music filtering out of the Palace. Will still had the uneasy feeling of someone watching his every move. They moved into a shadowed corner where they were out of view, but they could see through the large window into the saloon. Several people stood on the walk outside, talking loudly.

"This is it," Joseph said. "We wait here until we know she's upstairs."

The four men stood against the wall, listening to men drinking, arguing, and singing along with the piano player. Will kept a close eye on the women making rounds in the room. They teased one man after another, not staying with anyone for very long. Then he noticed Kate.

The beautiful blonde worked between the bar and the tables, scurrying back and forth with drinks and bottles. Will watched as men grabbed and groped at her, and the fire in his gut grew hotter and hotter. He could not accept that she was lost. He would do whatever he must to save her.

Sam poked at Will's arm, drawing his attention from the inside of the saloon to the street. "Look at that," Sam whispered.

Will saw Sheriff Gregory ambling toward the Palace, with one arm draped over Gil's shoulder.

"Now, I don't want to hear another apology from you," Gregory said. "Everyone makes mistakes sometimes."

The deputy scratched his head. "I know, but if I had been watching like you told me, they wouldn't have been able to start that fire in the first place. I just," Gil's voice faltered. "It won't happen again, Sheriff."

"I know it won't. It was an honest mistake. And Madame isn't holding it against you. Neither will I." Gregory's voice was emphatic. Too emphatic to be sincere.

Frenchie shook his head. "I doubt Madame is as forgiving as the sheriff suggests."

"Shh." Will raised a finger to his lips as the sheriff continued.

"You don't have to worry about a thing." Gregory patted Gil on the back. "And just to prove it to you, I have a little something special planned."

The two men entered the Palace, and Will strained to hear what was coming next. He saw Gregory take Gil to the bar and order drinks, and then the lawman leaned over the bar to say something to Redbeard.

A moment later, the room quieted as a new song peeled out from the piano.

Frenchie and Sam raised their brows.

"That is the song for Madame Boulay's special," Frenchie said. "She will be paid one thousand dollars in silver."

Will watched the scene unfold as his gut tightened. Juliette Boulay came down the grand stairway, wearing nothing but her stockings and the black ribbon at her throat. She again snaked between the tables as she crossed the room to where Gil stood.

Seeing it from the outside as it happened to someone else made Will's stomach flop and pitch bile into his throat.

Juliette reached out and pulled Gil's string tie with one hand, as she took a bag of silver from Gregory with the other. She led the blushing deputy back up the stairs as the crowd began to cheer.

Will's heart pounded as he saw the other four blood-sisters gather at the foot of the stairs. He assumed they would soon take their first round of men upstairs as well.

"It is time," Joseph said. He pointed to the back of the building. Stay in the shadows and keep to the outside edge of the stairs.

Frenchie led the way, and Joseph closed the procession with his gun drawn. Will and Sam hurried to keep pace. Will kept turning, still feeling as though they were not alone.

They reached the back stairs and began ascending silently. At the top landing, Frenchie looked inside to be sure nobody was guarding the door. He turned to the others with a nod. He pulled the door open, and without a sound, the men filed into the narrow hallway.

They inched their way in and waited for a moment, not wanting to be surprised by a day-walker or one of the other whores. Will handed Sam a stake, and all four men held their weapons ready to strike.

Before they could move, though, a creak sounded from the back stair door. The men froze in place, eyes wide. A slim shadowed figure stepped inside and closed the door behind him.

Joseph lunged forward and caught the man by the throat, pushing him against the wall and covering his mouth to keep him silent.

Will recognized him and let out a nervous sigh.

"Jack!" Sam whispered loudly. "What are you doing here?"

Joseph looked at Sam and Will with a knitted brow. "You know this young man?"

"Yes, you can let him go, but only if he swears to keep quiet," Will said in a warning.

Jack nodded, his eyes glowing white with fear.

Joseph released him, and Jack gasped for air. "I didn't mean to scare you," Jack squeaked. "I just wanted to help, too."

"You can't," Will uttered. "You don't have any weapons, and we've been preparing for this. It's too dangerous."

"But I have to help. This is my city, too." Jack's voice was barely audible. "I'm not too young to help."

Sam and Will exchanged a glance, unsure of what to do with the youth.

Frenchie shook his head. "We need to move now."

Will leaned close to Jack's ear. "You can be our lookout. We're going into Madame Boulay's room. If anyone starts to come in after us, you yell as loud as possible, and then you run out this door and go home. Don't look back. Don't wait for us. Do you understand?"

Jack's face looked pale in the dimly lit hallway. "Yes. I understand."

"Can you do that?" Sam asked. "You have to swear not to come in after us, no matter what you hear."

"And if Madame Boulay comes out, and we don't, you just run," Will added.

Jack nodded. "I swear," he whispered. He backed up against the wall with his hand within reach of the door handle.

Frenchie held up his stake and motioned forward. "Let us slay the beast; Godspeed to us all."

CHAPTER
TWENTY-SIX

The four men proceeded down the hall with cautious steps. They paired off, pressing their ears to the doors of each room, listening for any noise. One room, then the next. Silence, a headshake, and a gesture to the next door.

Will tried to stay quiet, tried to keep his nerves under control. He couldn't feel the pain that had racked his body just a few hours earlier. He couldn't think of anything but driving his stake between Madame Boulay's breasts. He wanted revenge for his mother and father. For Kate and Tiger. He wanted her dead.

He looked down the hall and realized they were coming to the room closest to the head of the grand stairs. The noise from downstairs was making it hard to hear anything behind the doors. If they got too close to the stairs, someone from below might see them. Too much could go wrong.

His heart slammed against his ribs, and his knuckles ached as he clenched his stake in his hand.

There were only three doors left facing the hall. He was ready. He hoped he was ready.

Will pushed his ear up to the next door and listened. A long, quiet moan rose from inside. Was it his imagination? Was it what he wanted or expected to hear? He lifted his ear, shook his head, and then pressed his head back into place—another moan.

He waved his arms to get the other's attention and pointed to the door and nodded.

He knew the plan. They all did. Go in, subdue Gil, surround Boulay, and stab the stakes into her. Keep stabbing until someone drove it through her heart. Will knew that the process would have to be repeated with each of the blood-sisters, but they would take it one at a time.

It was a good plan.

Joseph took the lead position at the door. As soon as he opened the door, they would all rush in. They knew the element of surprise was the key to their success. Each man nodded that they were ready.

Joseph threw open the door, and all of them ran inside. What they saw froze them in place.

Juliette and her four blood-sisters surrounded Gil in the center of the bed. They were naked, except for the sheen of scarlet that covered them from their lips to their knees. Gil was also nude and torn open from his neck to his groin. His genitals were missing, as were most of his organs.

The women were gorging themselves on his flesh and lapping up his blood from his skin and each other. So drunk were they in their revelry, they didn't even see the men come in.

Will's presence of mind returned, and he raised his stake over his head, unable to stand another minute of the orgy.

In one swift motion, he took a step and plunged his stake into the back of the woman closest to him. A sharp, second-long screech escaped her lips before she fell in a heap at the foot of the bed.

Frenchie and Joseph attempted to do the same, but the other four women now faced them with wild yellow eyes. The women seemed to change before the men's eyes. Their skin became an almost luminous blue, and they bared fangs like wolves. They lunged toward them, and the men tried to strike back.

It was all the men could do to avoid being bitten. They stabbed with all their strength but caught nothing but air. Joseph fired his revolver at one of the women, a bullet tearing through her shoulder, causing her to spin around. As she turned, Frenchie was able to land a blow with his stake into her side. It didn't penetrate her heart, but it gave Joseph the chance to run his stake through her. She dropped to the floor, dead.

Juliette, Lily, and the other woman seemed to rise from the floor, floating to the ceiling. As they moved toward the door, Frenchie called to the others, "We have to get out now. If they trap us inside the room, we won't get out alive."

Joseph shot again, missing Boulay and Lily, but hitting the other one in the leg. Sam fired his pistol as well but didn't hit anyone.

Will and Sam hurried out into the hall as Joseph and Frenchie followed. They raced to the door at the back stairs. Jack saw them coming and opened the door, running just ahead of them down the staircase.

Reaching the ground, the men looked around to see if the women followed them. They each drew another stake and prepared to strike again as they saw Lily and the other blood-sister floating down from above. Juliette Boulay was not with them.

The four men readied themselves for another attack, moving into position with their backs together, as Joseph had taught them. From the corner of his eye, Will saw that Jack was standing at the corner of the Palace, watching.

"Go home," Will called to him.

But Jack didn't move. Lily saw the boy and swooped down beside him. Before the men could make a move, she had sunk her fangs into Jack's neck. As she dropped his lifeless body, she let out an almost gleeful howl.

Fury burned in Will, and he rushed toward Jack. The other woman swooped at Will, but Sam took a shot at her, striking her in the side of the head. Though the bullet penetrated her temple, it slowed her only enough to allow Will to dodge her reach.

Will dropped to his knee and rolled away from her, allowing Frenchie to grab her by the arm and throw her to the ground.

The woman began kicking and clawing at Frenchie as he stabbed at her, over and over, until she stopped moving.

When Will looked up, he saw Sam hovering over Jack's broken body. Joseph stood looking up, with his pistol in one hand and a stake in the other, both hanging limp at his sides.

"Come to me, Lily," Joseph cried. "Take me with you, or let me take you with me."

Lily floated down beside him, and he stood there with tears on his cheeks, not raising either weapon. "Joseph," she purred, with Jack's blood still warm on her lips.

"I loved you," he said, raising his arm and burying his stake into her heart. He caught her body as she slumped forward and lowered her to the ground.

"I loved—" and her words faded into a death rattle.

CHAPTER
TWENTY-SEVEN

Will, Joseph, and Frenchie turned around, expecting to be surrounded by a mob of day-walkers, but there was no one else. From the first shot in the room to that moment had taken less than five minutes.

"He's gone," Sam said, still at Jack's side. For the first time since Will met him, Sam was at a loss for words.

"Find a safe place to hide him until we can take him to his mother," Will said. He shot a glance at Joseph and then Frenchie. "And stay with him, Sam. We don't know where Juliette is, and I don't want her getting to Jack."

Sam nodded without a word and picked up the limp body. In a few more seconds, he disappeared into a shadowed backstreet.

Something flickered overhead—a silhouette passed in front of the moon. Will looked up just in time to see Boulay soar above him, carrying another woman. Kate.

His stomach lurched as his heart pounded in his ears. All she had to do was let go, and Kate's body would be dashed apart on the rocky desert floor. Or sink her fangs into her neck and let her bleed to death. Or force her blood into Kate and steal her soul forever.

Will had witnessed Joseph's sacrifice and was sure he didn't have the strength to do the same.

"She's heading to your place," Joseph said. "We need to hurry."

Before any of them moved, that mob they expected before arrived from the front side of the Palace. Joseph and Frenchie stepped forward.

"Go, Will," Frenchie said, motioning toward the homestead. "We'll be along soon."

"Remember, brother," Joseph added. "Ten Skies gave you an extra measure of protection. Do not waste the gift."

Will saluted both his friends, watching them draw their pistols and knives on the crowd of men coming toward them. He hoped and prayed he would see them again.

He ran through the side streets, seeing no one else, hearing no other sound but his own heart pounding in rhythm with his footfalls. How would he face Juliette alone? What would he find when he met her? He had run away before. Would he run again?

No. This time Will had to stand up to her.

Another thought clouded his mind. Was this what his father had faced when she gave him no other option? He quickened his pace. He couldn't let Kate die—not like his mother.

His side ached as he approached the edge of the blackened earth. The charred remains of his home smelled bitter in his nostrils. Or maybe it was the witch.

In the moonlight, Will could see Juliette standing on the high point, where the house had once been. She wore a crimson dressing gown with a sheer chemise underneath. Her skin was pale, contrasting with her black hair and eyes.

Beside Juliette stood Kate in her green dress, looking bewildered. Will thought he saw her trembling.

He slowed when he saw that Boulay held Kate by the throat.

"Come on, boy. Don't be so shy." Juliette crooked a finger in his direction. "I think she'd like to see you again."

Will took slow steps toward the women. "Let her go, Juliette. Your fight is with me, not her."

"Juliette?" she asked. "Not Madame Boulay? And how did we become so familiar? Perhaps you're not as shy as I thought?"

"When you murdered my parents, you lost the respect of any title you might have claimed before."

"You think I care about respect?" She rocked her head back and laughed. "I don't need respect. But I demand fear."

"I don't fear you. Look around; I have nothing left for you to take."

She shrugged. "That's why I brought your darling Kate, my boy."

Will worried that he had overplayed his hand. He tried to work out his next move but could think of nothing else but Kate.

Juliette released her grip on Kate's neck, and Kate dropped to her knees in the ashes. "I know you don't want me, but I'm the only one who can give you her."

Boulay took a step back and held her palm up toward Kate. She curled her fingers upward, and Kate rose to her feet.

Will reached out to her, and Kate took a dozen steps in his direction. Slowly at first, then more confident as she closed the gap between them.

"I waited for you, Will," Kate's voice was low, dripping with sugar. "And now that you're here, we can have a perfect life together." She pushed the ruffles off of her shoulders and unfastened the top hooks on her corset. She took Will's hand and placed it over her breast in the same way Boulay had at the Palace. "This is what you want, Will."

It was what he wanted, but not this way. He drew his hand away from her and marched past her to face the witch.

"She's not like you, Juliette. She's a good woman. Respectable."

"Perhaps she's not like me yet, but she could be." Boulay held up her hand toward the city, and Will glanced in that direction. He saw Sheriff Gregory walking toward them. "I can make any person in this town do whatever I wish."

"Not out of respect." Will pointed toward the sheriff. "He's a prime example. He doesn't care about you at all. He cares what you can give him." Will's mind danced from one thought to another until he found a place to land. "Why don't you tell him when you're going to make him like you. He wants to live forever. When will you give him that?"

Gregory's attention piqued as Will spoke. He dipped his chin toward Boulay. "Madame, don't bother with this boy. He is nothing. Kill him and be done with it all."

Boulay glared at the lawman. "It's not your place to tell me what to do," she said. "I let you do things your way for long enough. You're worse than useless to me."

"Madame, I just thought," he began but faltered.

"You don't think at all. You want to be clever. You want to be a king." Boulay spat out her words like bile.

"I'd be king to your queen," Gregory answered.

Will reveled in the conflict. He moved slowly to draw a stake from his pouch, ready to strike at his first chance.

Boulay gasped. "A queen doesn't need a king." She flicked her wrist at Gregory. "A queen needs servants." She turned her attention back to Will. "And those who offer their fealty. Your father resisted his sacrifice. You'll do well not to follow his example—unless you wish to share his fate." She marched toward his parents' gravesites. "There is plenty of room for another grave."

Will swallowed hard, trying to breathe through his fear. Before he could answer, Will felt the gentle touch of Kate's hands on his shoulders.

"Please, William. Don't force her to destroy you. If you give in, you can have me."

It was Kate's voice, but the words were Juliette's. Will pushed her hands away. "Don't touch me, Kate. Don't make me hurt you. I don't want to, but I will."

"You couldn't hurt me, William. You love me." Kate's arms wrapped around his waist. "You desire me. And I can be yours."

Will pushed her away with all the strength he had. Without looking back, he took another bold step toward Juliette. "If you want to fight me, do it yourself. Don't use her body."

Gregory held up his hand to stop Will. "You stay away from her, Bancroft. You have no idea of her power."

"I do, Gregory. Do you?" Will said.

The sheriff huffed and drew his pistol in a fury. He held it level with Will's head. "You watch your mouth, Son."

"Put your gun away," Boulay said. "I'll deal with the boy."

"I can take care of him." Gregory's fist tightened around the grip. "Just give me one shot."

Boulay rolled her eyes. "You've become tiresome, Gregory. Take your one shot." She flipped her wrist in a shooing motion toward the sheriff.

Gregory's hand began to shake. He lifted the revolver to his head. "Please, no." His whole body shook. "Please."

"Juliette, no!" Will yelled.

It was too late. Gregory had pulled the trigger, blasting his brain out of his head. The sheriff's body dropped to the ground with a thud.

"You see, Bancroft, I can do whatever I like. I can take whatever I like." Boulay clicked her tongue. "Now you have a choice to make. Are you going to give me what I want, or do I have to take it? You cannot win, either way. But if you make the right choice, you can at least live." She waved toward the sheriff's body. "And who knows? Maybe someday I would like a king. You could live forever if I let you."

Will squinted his eyes, trying not to see the shattered half of Gregory's skull. "That's the problem, isn't it? You're not living forever, are you? You're dying forever."

"Close your mouth," Boulay screeched.

He let a curl form on the side of his mouth. "I'm not yours to order about, and I never will be." Will took another long step in her direction, and she took a step back.

"Stay where you are," Boulay said with a tremor in her voice.

"Are you afraid?" Will asked. "Because I know what you are?"

Boulay shook her head, and her black curls fell loose over her shoulders. "I'm not afraid of you." She raised her fingertips to her lips.

"You look like you're afraid." Will took another step.

Boulay flinched. "Please stay back," she whined.

"You aren't as powerful as you think you are," Will said, lunging at her with his stake aimed between her breasts.

She dodged his strike easily, batting the wooden stick from his hand and sending it into the darkness. She slapped at the side of his head, knocking him several yards away from her.

"Child!" Boulay's voice sliced through the cool night air. "You think you're smart. I've heard every last thing a man has to say. Scared, bold, angry. It doesn't matter. I can manipulate anyone. I can certainly manipulate you."

Will reached for another stake from his pouch, but the bag was gone. He looked around, thinking it was knocked off when he fell.

Boulay stood her ground—his ground—laughing again. Beside her stood Kate, holding his pouch of stakes like a prize.

"You see?" Juliette's smile was as bright as the moonshine. "I can take what I want from you." She walked to his side. "I didn't want to have to kill you. I'd rather enjoy you."

She dropped to her knees and clasped his left wrist in her hand. She pulled back his sleeve enough to see where she would make her mark.

Will felt his heart pounding. He couldn't let her take him. He raised his right knee, connecting with her temple, knocking her backward into a roll. "I guess I can lure you, too."

Juliette knit a string of curses that began in English, changed into French, and then into another language he never heard before. She rose from the ground a foot or two, her eyes glowing gold and her skin blue-white. "You are mine, boy!"

"You may see me as just a boy, but when I end you, you will

spend all eternity in hell knowing William Bancroft was a man standing up for what he believes." Will's voice sounded more confident than he felt.

Juliette grinned, baring long white fangs. "I can take any man as easily as I can take a boy."

"You cannot have me," Will shouted, rising to his feet.

"I have razed your father's house to the ground with your mother and him inside. I will have everything." Boulay dipped down at Will, reaching for his arm again.

With a quick turn, Will avoided her grasp and caught hold of her wrist, slashing with the knife he'd pulled from his boot when she wasn't looking.

She yanked back, but Will refused to let go. "Look here," he said, pointing to the ribbon of blood snaking from her arm. "What would happen if I drank this? I would have your blood inside of me." He licked his lips. "That would be interesting, wouldn't it? I wonder if I would control you?"

She yanked again, nearly pulling Will off the ground. "Let go of me," she cried.

"Don't do it, Will," Kate's voice floated to his ears. "It's evil. Please, don't. You're not evil. You're a good man."

Will knew that both of them were scared. Genuinely scared. He squeezed Boulay's arm tighter, part of him wanting to taste, as she had suggested before. He leaned closer to her arm,

"NO!" Kate screamed, running head-on into Will.

She knocked him to the ground, and he lost his grip on Boulay.

Boulay waved her arm at Kate, sending her crashing backward.

"Don't touch my woman again," Will shouted, struggling to regain his footing. The pain in his ribcage returned with a vengeance. He staggered upright, refusing to give in to it.

"She is mine, not yours," Juliette said. She swooped back to the ground and licked the stream of blood from her arm. She took another dozen strides away from him, gesturing toward the city.

"You have only a moment left with her. My servants are coming. See?"

Will tried to catch up with her, but as he looked over Juliette's shoulder, he saw them. At least a dozen men running toward them. He had to strike now. No more talk.

He looked down at his empty hands and patted them over his body. He had nothing to use against Juliette.

Will looked for his knife. It had been knocked from his hand when Kate had hit him, and it was lost in the blackness. He could see the pouch of stakes, but it was too far away to reach before the day-walkers would be upon him.

Boulay sauntered toward the approaching crowd like a queen receiving her court. She raised her arms into the sky and cackled. Turning back to Will, she smirked. "I will call the depths of hell upon you. I will dance on your parents' graves as my slaves dine on your flesh."

"Then I will take you with me," Will cried, racing to grab her arm again. She pushed him away as though she were swatting a fly, and he fell down upon his father's burial.

"I'm sorry, father. I have failed again." Tears flooded over Will's cheeks as he looked up and saw his mother's name scrawled out on the wooden grave marker.

Will scrambled back to his feet as the crowd neared.

"You should give up, boy," Juliette said with a matter-of-fact tone.

"I surrender," he said, staggering toward her. He held out his left wrist for her. "Just be quick."

She smiled, taking his wrist and drawing him close. As she opened her mouth for her first bite, Will raised his right arm. He brought down the cross into her chest in one stroke, not stopping until his mother's name no longer showed.

As she dropped to the ground, Will turned away to face the rush of day-walkers. At the front of the crowd, he saw Frenchie and Joseph, running at top speed, away from the others.

CHAPTER

TWENTY-EIGHT

Joseph and Frenchie raced to Will's side, forming a wall against the mob, still charging their direction.

"Stop!" Will shouted. His voice echoed in the emptiness of the dark night sky. "She's dead. And if *she* can die, *you all* can."

Will gestured to the Madame's body, lying face-up across the burial mounds, with Mary's marker cross still impaled in her chest.

"What did he say?" multiple people asked at the same time as they slowed at the sight of the body in the moonlight.

"He said that Madame Boulay was dead," others murmured.

"The sheriff, too," yelled another voice.

The crowd gathered around the bodies of Boulay and Gregory. "All the Palace women are dead," Will heard Jacobs say through a wheeze. The round man's face was flushed from running, and he bent over, bracing his hands on his knees, gasping for breath.

Albert Sanderson stared at the woman for several long minutes. His expression was a strange mix of consternation and relief. "Someone finally did it. She's gone." And without another word, he turned around and walked back toward town.

One man after another stepped up to see the bodies, muttered something, and then walked away. Will faced no other challengers.

Will turned away from the bodies, searching for Kate. She sat on a pile of rubble, pulling at the hooks on her corset, trying to cover herself. When she saw Will coming, she dropped her head to her chest, sobbing.

Taking a seat on the ground beside her, Will reached for Kate's hand. "Are you all right?" he asked.

She pulled her hand back. "No, I want to die." Kate sounded like a child, her tone round and high, like the young girl Will remembered.

"I can't let you die now," Will said. "I've worked too hard to keep that from happening." He reached his arm around her bare shoulder.

She pulled away. "Please, don't," she said. "Juliette almost killed you, using me to do it."

Will scooted away from Kate, shifting to face her. "And the only reason you were even in that situation is that I was the jackass who had to make a fortune before we could get married. If I hadn't left you here alone—"

"You can't know that it would have made any difference," Kate argued.

"For that matter," Will said, "she didn't kill me. In fact, when you ran into me, you saved me from doing something terribly stupid." He took her hand in his. "And even that first night in the Palace, it was you who saved me from Juliette. Why don't we start all over?"

This time Kate didn't pull her hand back. "What do you mean?"

Will cleared his throat and straightened his spine. He smiled and squeezed her hand. "Hello, Kaitlin. I'm back in town. I surely missed you. Will you marry me?"

Tears spilled over her cheeks, and she shook her head. "You don't want me, Will. I'm not the girl you remember."

He matched her tears and dropped his head. "Kate, you're all I want. You're the reason I came back to Virginia City. And you may be different than when I left, but so am I. And there's not a single thing about you that scares me. Well, that may not be entirely true. There are a hundred things about you that scare me, but that's how I felt when we were courting before." He smiled. "Will you at least allow me to court you again?"

Kate nodded and fell into Will's embrace. "Yes, Will Bancroft. You may court me again."

Will looked up to see a wagon had arrived, driven by a couple of men with torches. He nodded toward them. "I'd better see what's happening."

He stood and helped Kate to her feet, and the two of them walked wearily back to where Frenchie and Joseph stood. The men on the wagon seat both wore deputy badges, and in the back of the wagon were the bodies of the other four Palace women. The deputies climbed down to pick up Boulay and Gregory.

Will glanced at the bodies for only a second, feeling both proud and sickened by what he had done. Gregory's body looked as it had before, but Boulay looked different. Her skin had shriveled into a gray shell as if she had been dead for ages, and her black hair was now white.

One of the deputies started to pull the stake from her chest, but Frenchie stopped him. "Leave it," he warned. "It is the only way to be sure."

The deputy offered a somber nod and waved a finger at the ragged troupe. "There are too many bodies here to ignore, I'm afraid. Someone will have to answer."

Will looked at Joseph, Frenchie, and Kate. He shook his head and took a step forward. Before he could say anything, Frenchie pushed him back to Kate's side.

"It was me. I killed them all." Frenchie nodded. "You should put me in jail. They tried to stop me, but my rage was too much."

"No," Will started. "You can't do this."

"See? He is still trying to stop me." Frenchie held up his hands in surrender. "Deputy, I can prove it was me. I am living in a little mining cottage. I have stolen some of Madame's clothing, and it is in my house. I will show it to you."

"You're confessing?" the deputy asked.

"I am. And there are two other murders, too." Frenchie nodded, turning to salute both Will and Joseph before continuing. "At the Palace, the man called Gil. And a boy. What was the boy's name?"

Will swallowed hard. "His name was Jack."

"Yes, Jack." Frenchie climbed up to the wagon's seat between the lawmen. "I think that is all of them."

Will, Kate, and Joseph watched the wagon roll away, leaving them in the dark. A slow creak sounded behind them, and all three whirled around to see the trap door to the cellar open. A dark figure emerged, and Will pushed Kate behind him. Joseph drew his pistol.

"Who's there?" Will called out.

"It is Ten Skies, Bancroft. I came to guard your home." The medicine man shook his head and approached them.

Joseph lowered his weapon and dropped the gun back into the holster. "Uncle, I might have shot you."

"What are you doing with guns?" Ten Skies asked. "Those aren't the weapons to fight demons."

Will clasped wrists with Ten Skies. "I, for one, was sure glad he had them."

"I kept your cellar safe," the older man said. "But you should build a house soon. It is stuffy in that little room, and your wife deserves a nice place to live."

"I agree." Will let out a deep sigh of relief. The action caused his ribs to ache again. He held his hand to his side. "I only wish..." his voice trailed off.

"If wishes were horses," came Sam's voice, as he led Tiger back to Will. "Look who I found loitering around the newspaper office."

The horse nosed Will's side and pawed at the ground with a timid snort.

Will threw his arms around his friend's thick neck. "I forgive you, Tiger."

Ten Skies nodded at them all and began walking away. He stopped and turned back for a second. "And if anyone needs any curses lifted, I will be at the river."

EPILOGUE

As I mentioned before, the story sounds too ridiculous to be true. No even-tempered contemporary would believe in such tall tales, no matter who told them. The fact that I, a confessed fabricator, would even attempt to plead honesty should raise reasonable doubt. But I will testify in the most upright and respectable court of law, on a stack of holy books, that what I witnessed and conveyed in this book is genuine.

The idea that monsters, witches, and devils might roam the world today is unfathomable. Terms like blood-sister, day-walker, or demon of air should be laid away in dusty tomes and relegated to old wives' tales. That a woman with such lust in her heart for silver and blood would shackle her very soul to the gates of hell is illogical.

But believe it, or doubt at your own peril.

What I know for sure, and perchance you'll consider worthy of repeating, is that there are still men in this world who will fight for their family's honor. They will battle the legions of darkness for the love of a good woman. There exist to this day a class of character willing to lay down their lives so that others may enjoy freedom and a good name.

I can relate, too, that Frenchie—Alois, rather—went proudly to the gallows, never ceasing to boast that he had the blood of Madame Juliette Boulay on his head. Redbeard, whose name turned out to be McConnell, returned to his position of owner and manager of the Palace Saloon.

Ten Skies and Joseph now act as liaisons between the citizens of Virginia City and the Shoshone settlement. Tensions often run high, but raids in either direction are few and far between.

Will Bancroft married the lovely Kate, and they now have a babe arriving shortly. Their silver mine is still producing, and they both enjoy a highly respected place in society. And, perhaps most importantly, Tiger is thriving and popular, occasionally leading the local parades.

I have bid farewell to my desk at the Territorial Enterprise, on my way to a position in San Francisco. I expect to have a few more stories to share in the future, besides my news articles. However, after this fantastical adventure, I hope to pen tales of purest fiction.

THE END

About the Author

Irwin Black was raised in a small Texas town and is a country boy at heart. He's a family man who spoils his wife every chance he gets.
He loves history, music, travel, and people-watching.
For more information, and to find out what's next for Irwin Black, visit his website: www.irwinblack.com.

instagram.com/irwinblackauthor